MY DRAGON MATE

MISTVALE
SPIN-OFF

STELLA RAINBOW

Contents

Dedicated to:
Cameron, for giving me so many plot bunnies that I need new notebooks to store them all.
Cassie, for making William, Raiden, and Cam's story so much better.

One

William

The fear kept me home. It had since we'd first been told that Camille wouldn't survive.

Thankfully, I'd heard some rumors around the children's hospital that magic existed in this world. It took a little hard work and maybe a less-than-moral deed to convince one such magical being, a mage, to heal my daughter, but Raphael Woodward ended up being a God-send. I owed him everything.

Even though he'd assured me time and again that my daughter was completely healed, completely healthy, I was still scared. I was scared that one day I'd wake up, and she would be gone, just like her mother.

But Cam was healed, and I knew I needed to get back to work. *But how?*

Every time I thought about going back to the office, panic started clawing up my throat, choking me. What if something happened to my daughter and I wasn't there?

That was why I was now seated across from Raiden Raine, one of my top investors. I'd never met the man before, and if it weren't for the fear, I'd have never been so unprofessional as to invite him to my home for a meeting. Especially when it looked like the storm outside would only get worse.

"I don't think it would be safe to venture out in that," I commented as I stared out the window. The rain was pelting down hard, with lightning flashing every few seconds. Mistvale saw a lot of rain, but there were rarely any storms, especially ones this bad.

Raiden followed my gaze outside, his gray eyes an almost perfect replica of the storm-darkened skies. He had the whitest hair I'd ever seen, so pale it gleamed in the bright overhead lights, momentarily giving him a halo. Raiden was in his early forties, and even though I was as straight as they came, I could see why heads turned when he walked into a room, why Rose—Cam's nanny and our housekeeper—had kept stuttering when she'd brought him a cup of coffee. He had this appeal, this weird draw that pulled people in.

I rolled my eyes at the fanciful thoughts running through my head. What did I know about gorgeous men, anyway? He's just a pretty face and one hell of an investor.

"I don't think the rain will be too much trouble," he murmured, his voice barely audible over the storm.

"Are you kidding me? You'll end up in a crash with the way the storm is right now. How about you stay here until it lets up a little? Have dinner with us?" I realized my error as the words left my lips. Why the hell was I inviting a practical stranger to have dinner with me and my daughter? What the fuck was wrong with me? First, I hadn't wanted to go back to work, and now I was asking a stranger to eat at our table.

Come to think of it, I'd made some terrible decisions over the last few weeks, but those decisions were the reason Cam no longer had leukemia. However, what I did to Raphael to make that a reality was right up there with inviting a stranger to have dinner with my daughter and me. God, someone needed to stop me before I made any more bad decisions. I needed a break.

Raiden stared at me with a raised brow, probably trying to figure out if my offer was genuine. Well, I wouldn't take it back, no matter how stupid it had been in the first place.

"Thank you. I'd like to have dinner with you," Raiden said in the same soft voice, and I wasn't sure if it was my imagination, but I could swear I heard him add "I think."

Raiden

William told me the housekeeper would be around with a drink before leaving to take a shower, and I breathed a sigh of relief. Whatever cologne that man wore had made my nose itch the moment I stepped into his house. It had taken all my years of self-control and a little help from my magic to keep from sneezing in his face during our meeting. Hopefully, he'd skip the cologne after his shower.

The housekeeper, Rose, a young woman with a polite smile on her face, came by with an offer for a variety of drinks, but I just asked for a glass of water. My magic had been going haywire since this morning, and I could not understand what was wrong with it. It caused the storm all over Mistvale, and I wished I could figure out why so I could get things under control.

I sipped my water as I stared out the vast stretch of glass windows. What was wrong with my magic? It had been perfectly fine before I left for work this morning. Over the course of the day, the rain had turned from a gentle shower to a full-blown storm, and I couldn't bring it under control, no matter what I tried. I was a dragon for mother's sake. I had two thousand years of experience. This should be easy for me, but it seemed like my magic had a mind of its own today.

My head snapped toward the hallway when I heard footsteps, and my eyes widened the merest bit when they fell on the little girl. It didn't take me long to realize she was William's daughter. What was her name again? Camille!

"Hello there, you must be Camille," I greeted her with a wave and a soft smile. I'd been told repeatedly by my advisers that I intimidated new clients, so I attempted to relax my shoulders and uncross my arms. The last thing I wanted to do was to scare off a child.

"I am. What's your name?" she asked as she swung a tennis racket around. She frowned as she stared out the window, and I got the feeling she wanted the rain to stop. *Me too, little one.*

"My name is Raiden Raine, and it's lovely to meet you."

Camille gave me a nod and said, "Hello, Mr. Raiden." I opened my mouth but she continued, "I had cancer. That's why Daddy works at home now. He's scared it will come back. It won't, though." The firmness in her voice had me smiling.

I'd heard she'd just defeated cancer. Since I knew everything that happened in this town—after all, for all intents and purposes, it was my town—I knew the Woodward mage had healed her. I'd never heard of healers like him before, but I guess in this constantly evolving world, it wasn't a surprise that magic was evolving too. I'd seen so many changes over the course of my long life that it hardly surprised me.

She skipped to the armchair and sat before pulling her feet into the seat and lounging back. She charmed me with stories of her late mother. Of how the woman had loved tennis, gardening, but disliked boats.

I crossed my legs and rested my chin on my palm as she spoke, her whimsy settling the brewing storm. I was a little in awe of her comfortability with me, a practical stranger, because attending staff meetings sometimes seemed too daunting a task for me, and I was a dragon with centuries of experience under my belt.

"Camille, what are you doing out here?" William's voice called from the doorway and I froze. Not because I'd been talking to his daughter when I should've clearly kept my distance, but because he had forgone his cologne, just like I'd hoped he would. And now, I could scent him clearly, despite the distance between us.

Everything made sense now. Why my magic had been acting up and why I'd had this weird feeling all day . . . why I couldn't seem to take my eyes off the green-eyed businessman I'd just met.

I'd recognize that scent anywhere. The scent I'd never expected to be graced with after spending the last two thousand years alone. It was the scent of mate. William was my mate.

Two

William

Dinner passed by with little fanfare or awkwardness.

When Cam got sick, we started having dinner much earlier because she tired easily. Now, even though she was healthy, our bodies had gotten too used to the schedule to give it up.

Raiden questioned nothing, though. He just ate quietly as Cam chattered between bites about anything and everything that came to her mind from her seat at the head of the table. Usually, I loved listening to her talk over dinner, but today, I kept getting distracted by the man sitting across from me.

It seemed like every time I looked up, his intense gray eyes trapped me. His head tilted to the side like a predator watching its prey. It unnerved me a little, to be quite honest. I wasn't sure what had changed between our meeting and now, but something had.

After dinner, Cam headed back to her room to finish her homework. I'd homeschooled her for the past two years, though studying hadn't really been all that important in her life for some time. She was getting back to it now though, and come spring, she'd be going back to public school.

"Is something wrong?" I asked after we were back in the living room. The storm was still going strong, and there was no way it'd be safe for him to leave just yet. Was that what he was worried about? Did he not want to stay?

"No, not at all. Why?"

I shrugged, not sure how to go about telling him I'd caught him staring at me one too many times.

"William . . . Raphael Woodward healed your daughter, right?"

My guard went up the moment he said Raphael's name. Few knew who—and what—he was, and he'd trusted me with his secret. I needed to be careful about what I said.

"Yes," I answered simply and waited.

"So, you know things beyond the ordinary exist in this world?" The look in his eyes intensified, and I found myself unable to look away. They were . . . captivating and continually changing, the swirling colors matching the storm clouds outside.

I shook my head to clear my vision. I *did* know that. Raphael had taught Cam and me about the supernatural world only because he was healing her at the time; otherwise, he was forbidden to reveal himself to humans with the exception of his fated mate, his semnyar.

So, what was Raiden's question about? Was he a suspecting human or a supernatural himself? And how was I supposed to figure that out?

"What do you mean?" I played dumb.

"I mean you know Raphael is a mage, right? He should have told you before healing Camille."

I narrowed my eyes at him, knowing there could be only two ways this could go. "Are you a supernatural too, or did Raphael heal you or someone you know?"

"The first one. I'm . . . a dragon."

My eyes widened at his words, and if it wasn't for the serious set to his face and the intense look in his eyes, I'd have thought he was joking.

"A dragon? Like those creatures in the fantasy books who breathe fire and hoard things?" I couldn't keep the incredulousness out of my voice, even though he looked too tense to be lying.

"A dragon? Can I see?" A voice I knew all too well piped up, and we both looked up to see Cam's head poking around the doorway.

"Were you snooping on us, little one?" Raiden asked, a smile lighting up his face.

Cam blushed as she walked into the room and shrugged. "Please, Mr. Raiden, I've always wanted to see a dragon."

Raiden glanced at me and I shrugged. I didn't fully believe him yet, not because I thought he was lying, but because . . . dragons! Even so, I couldn't say no to my daughter, especially when she looked at me with her mother's big blue eyes.

"Okay then." Raiden smacked his thighs before rising. "Do you have a balcony we can get to? I haven't taken my true form in quite some time, and I'm not sure if I'd fit in the confines of the house the first time around."

I blinked as I processed his request, then nodded. Cam hurried out of the living room and up the stairs before hopping impatiently at the top.

"Alright, wait here a minute, please?" Raiden asked once we were upstairs, standing in front of the french doors that lead to the balcony. "I'll need to remove my clothes before I turn."

Cam and I nodded simultaneously. He smiled at us before sweeping the heavy pearl-gray curtains aside and walking out. There was a white canopy strung over half of the inordinate marble balcony, so at least the still dark and churning storm wouldn't drench him. I closed the doors and drew the curtains, then watched Cam as she counted down the two minutes while bouncing on the balls of her feet.

I still wasn't completely sold that the owner of the largest investment firm in the surrounding towns just happened to be a dragon, but I wouldn't say anything to make that smile on my daughter's face disappear. I just hoped Raiden wouldn't either.

Cam was grinning widely as she looked up from her watch. With the countdown over, she threw open the curtains and grabbed both door handles. That's when realization struck me hard.

Why had Raiden told me he was a dragon? Who was I to him? I couldn't be . . . right?

Camille

My eyes widened the moment I stepped out onto the hidden balcony. I was suddenly grateful that our home overlooked the woods at the edge of Mistvale and wasn't surrounded by nosey neighbors.

Because . . . wow . . . the dragon was enormous. He would have to dip his massive horn-covered head just to fit under the canopy that was rolling wildly in the wind. He stared down at me with those beautiful eyes, the gray colors in them whirling like the storm. He. Was. Beautiful.

I took a step closer, wanting to reach out and touch the rain-slicked, shiny blue and silver scales that interlocked to cascade down his body like armor. They reflected the brooding clouds above and glinted on the edges like knives.

In the books, there were different types of dragons. Wind dragons, fire dragons, storm dragons. Was Mr. Raiden a storm dragon? I'd have to ask him later.

I took a step closer to him.

"Close enough, Camille!" Daddy called out, but I waved him off. The dragon had been standing stone-still, as if he wanted me to see that he wouldn't hurt me. I wasn't scared of him.

I took another careful step, and just as I reached the end of the canopy that shielded me from the rain, the dragon raised one of his massive wings over my head. I looked up at the gray leather-like skin and grinned. He was such a sweetheart. I walked under the length of his wing until I was at his side.

His huge head circled down, and a puff of air flapped my hair and shirt as he sniffed me. When I giggled, he stuck out his tongue and I could see his teeth, sharp and bone white. With glee, I reached out a hand, then paused. "Can I touch you, beautiful dragon? Can you understand me like this?"

The dragon nodded his big head, almost knocking me to my butt, and I giggled again. Slowly, I raised one hand and placed it on the skin of his belly. It was warm and soft, but not like fur. It was like one of my mom's old, well-worn leather book covers.

Then, I touched his chin, gasping as my fingers brushed the thick leathery hide. He had thin pebbly lips and smooth scales that lined his jaw like a short beard.

"Daddy, come here!" I called out to him when I realized he was still standing in the doorway, watching us with a frown.

I didn't like that frown. I hated it. When I'd been sick, he'd stopped smiling. And when he'd tried to smile at me, I could see he was lying. That frown had always been there on his face when he thought I couldn't see it and I. Hated. It.

I was healthy now, and I didn't want him to ever be sad again.

"Can you do something to make my daddy smile, sweet dragon?" I whispered.

He stared at my daddy for a moment, and the storminess of his eyes settled. I opened my mouth to encourage him, but he shifted on one large claw-tipped, hand-like foot, his tail shooting out to curl around my daddy's waist. The long scales on the end of his tail flared as the dragon lifted Daddy from the ground and floated him across the balcony before placing him gently beside me. The tail uncoiled from around Daddy and appeared to slither away. I laughed at the look of awe on my daddy's face as he stared up at Mr. Raiden's Dragon, whose nose seemed to wrinkle in amusement too.

Then, the dragon covered us with his wings and tucked his head into the gap, surrounding us in the warmth of his body and the smell of leather and storms. It was perfect. Especially when my eyes met Daddy's, and he gave me a bright, genuine smile.

Yeah, it was pretty perfect.

Raiden

Sheltering the two of them with my wings, my magic cocooning us in its warmth, I felt better than I could've imagined. They felt like family, like home. I didn't know what I'd do if William rejected me, because I'd already started getting attached. I couldn't blame myself for it, though. I'd waited two thousand years for this connection. I deserved to be a little hasty.

"Alright, let's get inside. Poor Raiden is getting soaked," Will said, his voice firm as he gave Camille a look. My heart warmed at the worry in Will's voice. He cared.

Camille looked up at me with her big blue eyes and nodded. "Sorry, Mr. Raiden."

I wanted to tell her that there was nothing to apologize for and that the rain didn't bother me because it was a part of me, but she was already rushing off as soon as I opened my wings. Will smiled at me before following his daughter and closing the door behind him, though I'd seen something else in his eyes.

Confusion? Unease?

Had he understood why I'd told him this? And did he not . . . like the idea? Like me?

I quickly took my human form and dressed in the clothes I'd hung on the back of the patio chair under the canopy. The dress shirt immediately absorbed the rainwater from my skin, soaking it through and causing it to cling to my body. My slacks didn't fare much better.

Will was pacing in the hallway while Camille was nowhere to be seen. He looked up when I stepped inside, and his eyes roamed over my see-through shirt before he shook his head and met my eyes.

"You look different . . . younger," Will stated.

"Aw, yes. This body feels more natural to me. I only age myself as to not draw suspicion from those I work with, like yourself," I explained. It was the first step toward telling him who I was to him, who *he* was to me, and I felt a nervousness unlike I'd felt in centuries.

"You look twenty."

"Twenty-five."

Will raised a hand before letting it drop back to his side. "More on that later. Tell me, Raiden, why did you reveal yourself to me and my daughter? Why are you no longer worried about 'drawing suspicion'?" The cautious tone to his voice told me he'd figured it out—or at least had a suspicion—already. My heart sank as I realized the idea did not bring him the same joy it had brought me. He didn't want me.

Now that I thought about it, it made sense. Why should he want me? He had a beautiful daughter, a family. I was a loner, had always been, and he knew almost nothing about me. But why did I get the feeling he wasn't interested in getting to know me?

"I think you know, William."

"I . . ." He ran his fingers through his dark hair, leaving it to stick up in all directions. He was in his early forties and ruggedly handsome. His broad shoulders and thick chest pulled me in even before I realized he was my mate. His green eyes were bright as he watched me, but not happy. I remembered the look in Camille's eyes when she'd asked me to make her daddy smile. My mate had been through a lot in his short life and had seen a lot of pain. I did not wish to give him more. If that meant giving up on him, then I'd do it. His happiness meant more to me than anything. I would rather accept a lonely life for another thousand years than force him to spend them with me if that wasn't his wish.

"Do you not wish to be my mate?"

William stopped his pacing to look at me, his brows furrowing. "I've never . . . I've never been with a man. I'm straight. Are you sure you're my mate?"

Was that the problem, then? My gender? As a dragon, I was male but I wasn't limited to a male human form.

"I'm a dragon, William. I can turn into anything. Take any form. If you wish for a female mate, I can be that for you."

Will scratched his beard and shook his head, making my heart drop. No, it wasn't my gender. It was just me. He didn't wish to be my mate.

I nodded once, swallowing hard. I'd had two thousand years of practice hiding my emotions, but it was still a difficult feat to keep my eyes from watering and my voice from breaking as I spoke.

"It's alright. I understand. I don't wish to cause you any discomfort, William," I said as I turned away from him and toward the stairs. I needed to get away from here because my heart wanted me to sink to my knees and beg William not to reject me. But this was his wish. And I didn't want to hurt him.

He was still my mate though, even if he didn't want me. And I'd keep him and Camille safe, even if I couldn't be a part of their family. They were a part of my hoard now, and any dragon worth his salt would protect his hoard and keep it safe until his last breath.

"I'll let myself out. And don't worry, the rain won't hurt me. It's a part of me."

I rushed down the stairs before he could protest. He was a kind man. He'd ask me to stay, even if it made him uncomfortable.

As I stepped out into the rain, I looked up at the sky, at the dark clouds, and closed my eyes. Had the storm been a premonition? Had my magic been trying to warn me all this time? Had it known I was about to get my heart broken?

My tears were washed away with the rain, and lightning shot across the sky, breaking it into a million pieces just as my heart shattered. Poetic, eh?

Three

Camille

Oh, Daddy. You stupid, stupid man.

I knew I shouldn't call my dad stupid, but well, he was.

And I knew I shouldn't have been snooping on their conversation again, but it was clear they needed my help.

I sneaked off to my room as quietly as I could, not wanting dad to realize I'd heard everything.

I'd guessed who, or rather what, Raiden was to my dad, of course.

During our many healing sessions, Mr. Magician, aka Raphael, had told me a lot about his magic and the supernatural world. He said that the only humans who could know were those he healed and his mate.

That meant Mr. Raiden could only tell us about his dragon if he was my dad's mate because he's not a healer like Raphael.

Their conversation had just confirmed it.

The only difference between them was that my daddy still kinda loved my mom, and he thought gender was a good reason to reject his mate. I didn't know a lot about the kind of love Dad had shared with Mom, but I knew a fair share about the bond between mates.

I'd seen how miserable Raph had been without his mate close by. The first few days he was here to heal me, he'd been all alone. Then later, I met Jai and their love was something warm that I could feel on my skin like sunshine.

I wanted that happiness for my daddy. He'd been hurt enough times in his life that he deserved all the happiness he could get. My grandparents had died when Daddy was a teenager, and then Mom died too, and then I almost died. He'd been hurt way too many times. I wouldn't let it happen again.

I grabbed the phone Daddy had gotten me when I was sick, so I could talk to my school friends, and dialed the number of the only person I knew who could help.

"Cam! What's wrong? Are you okay?"

I face-palmed when I realized how late it was. But this was important. It couldn't wait.

"Hey, Raph. I'm okay. I need your help. Daddy found his mate who is this beautiful dragon, but then my daddy kinda rejected him? Because he's a guy, and then he left. But I don't want Daddy to be hurt again, and I want him to be happy with Mr. Raiden, like you are with Jai. Will you help me? Please? Please? Please?"

"Whoa, hold up. Let me get this straight. William's mate is a fu—reaking dragon, and William rejected him? Is he crazy?"

"I think so. Raiden looked really sad when he left too. He said the rain was a part of him, though. What's that mean?" I asked. I'd been curious about it when he said it, but I'd forgotten about it over everything else.

"Aha! So that's why this town has such crazy rain. He's a storm dragon, sweetie. I believe he controls the skies in this place."

"Ooh, like Thor!"

Raphael laughed. "Yes, just like that. Now, how about you hand over the phone to your daddy, and I'll try to talk some sense into him?"

"Okay!"

I hopped off the bed and rushed across the hall to Daddy's room. The door slammed against the wall in my hurry, and Dad looked up at me with wide, worried eyes.

"Cam? Are you okay?" he asked, immediately getting off the bed and rushing toward me. I nodded hastily, hating that I'd worried him again.

I pressed the phone into his hand and waved at it. He gave the screen a puzzled look before pressing it to his ear. "Hello?"

"You idiot!" Even I heard Raphael's voice through the phone. I grinned as I turned around and walked out of the room and closed the door behind me.

My work here was done.

William

"What?" I asked, completely confused as to why Raphael was calling me an idiot. He had reasons enough to swear at me, but why was he doing that now?

"Do you know what Cam just told me? She told me you rejected your mate—who is a fucking dragon—because he's a guy. You know dragons can change forms, right? He'd have taken the form of a woman within seconds if that's what you wanted."

"It's not that," I tried to explain, but it was difficult because I didn't know why I'd said that to Raiden either. I liked him as much as I could in the short time I'd known him. And that moment when he stepped inside, shirt sticking to his chest? I'd definitely felt something. Why hadn't I told him that, then? Why had I rejected him?

"Is this because of Avery?"

"Avery? What does she have to do with this?" Avery was my PA, but I couldn't for the life of me figure out what Raphael meant by that.

"Huh. I could've sworn there was something between the two of you."

I snorted at the idea of anything happening between me and my very lesbian PA before shaking my head. "She's just my assistant, Raphael. She works for me, that's it."

"So, what's the problem, then? Why the fuck would you reject your mate—who is a dragon—if you aren't hung up on someone else?"

"Why are you so hung up on the fact that he's a dragon?" I joked, even as my mind got stuck on what he'd said. Was that it? Was my heart still hung up on someone else? Not Avery, obviously, but Veronica?

It had been six long years since she died. I was over her, right? The ache in my chest said otherwise.

There was some shuffling on the other side of the phone before a different voice spoke. "Hey, Will. It's Jai."

"Hello, Jai," I murmured, surprised he wanted to talk to me. After what I'd done to Raphael, he'd been less than friendly toward me, which was completely understandable. It was also why the soft tone of his voice surprised me.

"It's Veronica, isn't it?"

I sighed, wondering how he'd figured that out so easily when it had taken me all night to come to that conclusion. "I believe so."

"I get it, William. When I met Raph, I didn't want anything to do with him because I knew my time was limited. I tried to stay away, but it just doesn't work like that. We were put together by Fate for a reason and so were you two. You know Veronica would just want you and Cam to be happy, right? It's clear Cam wants your mate to be a part of your lives. You don't have to just bond with him straight away. You can start off as friends, and I bet you'll figure it all out in time."

I thought over his words, knowing he was right. Before she'd died, Veronica had made me promise her that I would be happy, that I would find love. Would Raiden be that person, then? And was I ready for that?

I'd spent the last six years focused on my daughter and my business. It had been the way I coped, my escape from the loneliness I felt without Veronica by my side.

Was it time for me to get back to living? And could I do that with Raiden? Would he even really want to after the way I'd rejected him?

Raiden

I wasn't sure what time it was when I finally made it home. I'd spent the last few hours just driving around on the rain-slicked roads. Even after I'd poured all my hurt and heartache into the storm, I hadn't felt better.

Now, I slumped on my bed, still dressed in my slightly damp dress clothes. I did the right thing, didn't I? It was clear William didn't want me. Whether it was because of who I was or what I was, I didn't know.

Whatever the reason, he'd rejected me and I needed to accept that. I'd spent two thousand years alone, so surely, I could survive the next hundred the same way, right? But what would I do once he and Cam were gone? Without the familial bond, they would never become part of my hoard or receive my immortally. They could have stayed safe and healthy and young for a long, long time. If William had only accepted me.

I hated this. I hated that I had to lose out on not just a mate, but a daughter too. And I didn't even understand why he'd rejected me. He'd said it wasn't because I was a man, but what else could it be?

I'd taken the form of a man when I first started living among humans. I'd always taken a male form because I was a male. But maybe I could take the female human form. Maybe my mate would accept me if I did that. Or was the rejection because of something else entirely?

I groaned loudly as I buried my face in my pillows. He didn't want me and that was that. I needed to stop thinking about the what-ifs.

My phone buzzed in my pocket, startling me. Now that it had, I realized it was digging into my thigh, so I pulled it out of my pocket and threw it on the bed. It was probably another work memo. I'd take care of it tomorrow.

I glared at the blinking green light on the corner of the phone. Why hadn't I turned that setting off?

"Ugh, alright. I'll check it out." I grumbled to myself as I unlocked the phone, then froze. It was a text message. From William.

My hands shook slightly as I opened the message. Cold crawled up my spine as I realized he'd pretty much written an essay. I took a deep breath for courage before jumping in.

Hawthorne: Hey, Raiden, it's Will. I'm sorry about the way I acted before. I didn't know what to say, I guess. I was overwhelmed, and I did it all wrong. The thing is I loved Veronica, Cam's mom. She died six years ago, and I thought I was over her, but maybe I'm not. But I don't want to . . . lose you. I know we don't know a lot about each other, but I want to get to know you. I just don't know if I'm ready for more. If you'd be willing to be patient though . . . maybe we could try? Start off as friends, maybe? And please, please know that I really don't mind that you're a man. I married Veronica straight after high school and I loved her. After her, I never thought about anyone else. But you . . . you're different, Raiden. And I like you for who you are. Please give me a chance.

It hadn't been me, then? He really hadn't rejected me?

I bumbled over the keys as I tried to reply, cursing at my fingers for being so clumsy.

Me: I've waited a long time for you. I can wait for more. As long as you need, Will. How about we go to the park tomorrow? You, me, and Camille?

Four

Camille

I chased the puppy around the park, feeling better than I had in years. It was such a good day, with the sun shining brightly. The angry storm from yesterday had all but disappeared, and I wondered how much of that was because a certain dragon was happier today.

The puppy, whom I'd named Snuffles because he snuffled a lot, ran up to me. I kneeled before him in the grass, and he immediately attacked my face with licks, making me giggle. Raiden had given him to me earlier today, telling me he was mine to keep if my dad didn't mind. But I had a feeling dad was in on the surprise by the shy and pleased smile that spread across his face at the sight of Sniffles under Mr. Raiden's arm when he showed up to take us to the park.

I glanced back at the blanket Daddy had laid out and smiled when I saw him talking to Raiden, their heads close to each other. Daddy finally had a smile on his face and were his cheeks . . . pink? I loved seeing him so happy. I was so glad I'd called Raphael last night. I wanted my daddy to be the happiest man on the planet. The smile on Raiden's face was just as bright, and watching them together made my heart feel fuzzy.

I wanted to sit between them and share that happiness, but I also didn't want to interrupt. As if he'd heard my thoughts, Raiden looked up. His smile brightened when he found me watching them, and he waved me over.

"Come on, Snuffles." I picked up the puppy because I didn't want him to get lost or hurt. He was so cute and cuddly as carried him over, floppy ears bouncing the whole way.

Raiden patted the space between them when I came closer and I smiled. When I looked at Daddy, he was smiling too. So, I splayed myself on the blanket, my head on Daddy's leg and my feet on Raiden's.

They continued talking with me cuddled up between them, Snuffles quietly snuffling on my chest. And it was the best day ever.

I was with my daddy, and he was smiling brighter than I'd ever seen him before. Soon, I'd have another daddy—I knew I would, I was sure of it—and I'd already decided what I'd call him.

He was my daddy's dragon mate.

So, he'd be DD, my dragon dad. All I had to do now was wait.

William

Raiden was nothing like I'd assumed he would be. Sure, he was a shrewd businessman and had an eye for investing that made him excel in his field, but he was a lot more than that.

Raiden was . . . sweet. He was gentle with Camille, and when he smiled . . . well, it made me forget where I was and what I was saying.

I was confused. Lord, was I confused! All my life, I'd never considered myself to be anything but straight. And now, I had a man as my mate, and I was actually feeling something for him. I wasn't sure if it was magic at work or if I just hadn't realized that I wasn't, in fact, straight.

What I did know was I was feeling things for Raiden, and it was freaking me the fuck out.

Veronica was my high school sweetheart, and I've loved her for as long as I could remember. Could it be that I'd always been bi? I'd fallen in love so early and my heart was so full. Could it just be that I never searched for other possibilities? Or was I only attracted to Raiden because magic had joined us?

"Are you okay?" Raiden's soft voice broke through my thoughts, and I looked up to find him watching me, a sad frown on his face.

I smiled at him, hoping my face wouldn't show the turmoil boiling in my mind. None of this was Raiden's fault, after all. He'd probably spent a long time waiting for his mate, and here he was now saddled with me. And the fact that he was a *dragon* wasn't even what I couldn't wrap my head around; it was the fact that he was a man. *Jeez.*

"How old are you?" I asked him, surprising us both. I hadn't meant to ask that out loud, but I couldn't stop wondering just how long he'd been waiting for me.

Camille, who had her head on my lap and her feet on Raiden's thigh, looked up at him too, her eyes lighting up with curiosity.

"Uh . . ." Raiden scratched the back of his head, eyeing me warily. Did he think I'd use his age as a reason to back out? Well . . . I couldn't really fault him for that, could I? I'd practically rejected him yesterday for no reason other than gender.

"Around two thousand, I think," Raiden said finally, looking like he was about to puke as he waited for my reaction.

I didn't need to do anything, though, because Camille shot up into a seated position, her bright blue eyes wide, mouth opening to make an O-shape. "Whoa! Two thousand years? Really? That's amazing! You must've seen lots of marvelous things in your life then, right?"

"I have," Raiden said with the soft smile that only Cam seemed to bring to his lips lighting up his face. "I spent the first five hundred or so years as a dragon, but after that, I slowly started walking among the humans by taking their form, observing them, and copying what they did. Humans seemed to be the closest species to dragons in intelligence, and I thought it seemed like a suitable form to take. Dragons are rare, and in my two thousand years, I've only encountered another of my kind once. I'd spent my dragon years alone, hatching out of my egg in an abandoned nest, so the idea of walking among humans, of interacting with them, had seemed . . . nice."

The pained loneliness in his light-gray eyes, the far-off look in them, pulled at me. This was a side of Raiden I hadn't seen yet. Granted, we'd only just met, so there was obviously a lot we didn't know about each other, but the way he spoke of his loneliness made my chest hurt for him.

I wanted to do something, reassure him somehow that he wasn't alone now, that he'd never be alone again, but I didn't know how.

I didn't need to worry, though, because Cam pounced on him, wrapping her small arms around his neck as she hugged him. "Don't worry, DD. You're with us now, remember? You don't have to be alone anymore."

When Raiden looked at me, his eyes glistened with tears. The sight of my daughter's arms wrapped around him, of the way he clung to her, swallowing repeatedly to keep the tears at bay, that was what did it. This man, this dragon, was meant to be a part of us, of my and Cam's little family.

And so what if he was a man? I was attracted to him. That was proven yesterday when my body reacted to Raiden walking in from the balcony, dress shirt cleaning to his gorgeous wet skin. Just because I'd never been with a man before, didn't mean I couldn't ever be with one, right?

A smile spread across my lips as I finally let myself believe that this was possible. That I could have this, a family with my daughter and my . . . boyfriend? My mate?

I would need time. I knew I would. I'd have to say goodbye to Veronica for real this time, and I wasn't sure I was ready for that. But one thing I was sure of, I wanted this. I wanted a family with these two, and I knew they'd both stand by me with all the patience in the world as I figured everything out.

Five

Raiden

"Are you sure you will be fine?" William asked, adjusting his tie for the third time as he looked into the mirror.

It had been three weeks since that day spent in the park, since we'd started to get to know each other. William was going back to work today after a long break, and I'd offered to babysit Camille for him. Honestly, I was looking forward to hanging out with Camille one-on-one. Because now that William had accepted me, she was an important part of my family too. I wanted to get to know her, and as much as I loved hanging out with William, I couldn't focus on Camille completely when he was around. But it was clear William was having a hard time letting go, and I understood his plight completely. I didn't know how he had handled everything alone, but I knew I wouldn't have been able to.

I approached him, resting my hand on his shoulder. Our eyes met in the mirror, and I gave him a reassuring smile. "I promise it will be okay. And if anything goes wrong, I will call you immediately. I promise I will protect her with my life, William."

He turned, searching my face before pushing out a long, audible breath and looking back at the mirror. I leaned closer and pressed the softest of kisses on his temple. We hadn't kissed yet, and as I'd promised William, I was completely fine going at his pace. But sometimes, I just couldn't resist, and I had sneaked in quite a few temple and cheek kisses by now. William never seemed to mind, and if I had to judge by the slight smile on his lips, he actually liked it when I kissed him.

"Daddy?" A voice called a moment before Camille popped into the room, her eyes lighting up when she spotted us. "You're not chickening out, are you?" she asked and I chuckled.

"I think he is," I admitted, grinning when Will glared at me in the mirror. I stepped back, putting some space between us, and turned to Camille. "How about you give him a good luck kiss? Maybe that would help."

Camille nodded before walking over to her dad and looking up at him. She tilted her head to the side, and there seemed to be some kind of silent communication between father and daughter because William immediately sank to his knees in front of her, and she wrapped her arms around him, pressing a hard kiss against his cheek. "I'll be fine, Daddy. Don't worry. DD will be here with me."

We still hadn't figured out what DD meant, but Cam was adamant that only she was allowed to know what the nickname meant. I didn't mind obviously. I loved the fact that she had a nickname just for me. It made me feel . . . accepted, like I was a part of the family. I was really grateful that Camille had accepted me so easily. I mean, I would have worked my ass off to prove myself to her if she hadn't, but the way she had let me into her life so completely warmed my heart. Now, if only William could do the same . . .

"Okay," Will declared with a huge sigh, "I'm ready." He pulled back from the hug and pressed a kiss to Camille's forehead before turning to look at me.

He cleared his throat. "Take care of her, Raiden."

I nodded. This was a big moment for him, and no matter how slow we were going in our relationship, it was clear that he trusted me because he was entrusting the safety of the one he loved most into my hands. And that meant a lot more to me than he'd ever know.

"Don't worry, Daddy. I'm gonna make DD watch a movie with me." The cheeky grin on Cam's face told me she was up to something, and her father seemed to have caught on too because he raised a brow at her.

"Oh? Any particular movie in mind?"

Camille's toothy grin widened, lighting up her face. "*How to Train Your Dragon.*"

William and I locked eyes with the same raised-brow expression. After a beat of silence, we both broke into peals of laughter, Cam's giggles joining in as I tried to take a breath and control myself. Mother, this girl knew just how to light everyone up.

When we'd calmed down considerably, Will got to his feet, dusting off the knees of his pants before straightening. He still had a slight smile on his face as he took a deep breath and checked himself out in the mirror one last time.

"Alright, time to go."

The three of us walked together to the front door, and just as William grabbed the doorknob, Camille lunged at her father, wrapping her arms around his waist. She wasn't as unaffected by him going back to work as she'd tried to show us.

William dropped his hands to her back and held her to him, our eyes meeting as he gave me a wobbly smile.

I stepped closer and placed my hand on Cam's head, running my fingers through her short hair. "Cam, sweetie, he won't be gone long, yeah? How about you give him one last good luck kiss, and then we can have some ice cream while we watch the movie, okay?"

Camille nodded against her father's stomach before pulling away and looking up at him. With his palms still on her shoulders, a silent conversation passed between them. Finally, William smiled at her, took a step back, gave me a nod, and opened the door. I watched him go a moment before closing it softly behind him.

Cam stood there for a moment too, her eyes on the door, before she whirled around and threw herself at me. I hefted her into my arms, and she buried her face in my neck, her small body shaking with silent sobs.

"Shhh, sweetheart, he'll be back soon. I promise."

I pressed a kiss to the top of her head and rearranged our plans for today. Cam needed some cheering up, and I knew just what would do the trick.

"A walk?" Cam asked, raising a brow up at me much like her dad often did.

"Yeah. I thought we could take Snuffles to the dog park and play with him for a bit."

Camille smiled, wrapped her arms around my waist and squeezed, then pulled back. "I'll go get ready. Wait for me!" She shouted the last part as she raced off to her room, and I shook my head, smiling. She was such a bundle of energy, and a part of me was glad I hadn't seen her when she'd been ill. Of course, if I had found them a few years ago, Camille wouldn't have gotten sick in the first place. Now that I considered her and Will a part of my hoard, my magic could keep them healthy and nourished for as long as I lived. Once I'd completed my bond with William, of course.

I pulled out my phone and shot William a text, letting him know we were headed to the park. Then, I made a call to check in with my assistant, who was handling everything so I could spend the day with my future daughter. Honestly, I already considered Camille mine, but I'd refrained from mentioning that to Will. I didn't want to say or do anything that would cause him to panic.

After Brenda had assured me everything was going smoothly, I ended the call. Just in time too, because a moment later Camille rushed into the room, dressed in dark jeans and a T-shirt with the image of a wand with the words "It's LeviOsa, not LeviosA" underneath it.

"I'm ready! I just need to grab Snuffles' leash and then we can go!"

I chuckled as she raced off toward the coat closet by the front door, calling for the dog as she went. I'd been worried when I'd gotten the dog for her, unsure if she'd like him. But she'd taken one look at the puppy and she'd been smitten by him.

"Come on, DD! Let's go!"

William

Returning home, I opened the door to the sound of laughter. Removing my shoes and placing them in their designated spot, I loosened my tie as I walked into the living room with a grin large enough to hurt my cheeks, but I couldn't stop myself from smiling at them.

Raiden and Camille were cuddled up together on the couch, Cam's head resting on Raiden's thigh, her legs hanging off the side of the couch, over the arm. They were watching some cartoon on the TV, but Raiden looked up the moment I walked in. He gave me a smile, and Cam followed his gaze and shrieked when she saw me.

"Daddy! You're home!"

And then my hands were full of an exuberant nine-year-old. Cam pulled at my jacket, telling me she wanted to hug me properly, and I heaved her up into my arms. Her legs wrapped around my waist, her arms encircled my neck, and she showered my face with kisses, chattering about her day in between.

I laughed and jerked away from her wet lips, without success, and it was a few minutes before I remembered the other person in the room.

I looked up to find Raiden watching us with a soft smile, though his eyes were . . . dull. Sad. Why did Raiden look sad? The idea didn't sit well with me, and I gave him a questioning look, tilting my head.

Raiden shook his head and swallowed once, giving me a shrug and a smile that missed genuine by a mile.

"Um, I guess I'll get going," Raiden said softly, and Cam froze in my arms and pulled her face away from my neck, turning around to look at Raiden.

"You're not staying for dinner?" Cam asked him as I set her down, and he shrugged again, shaking his head.

"Um, no. I thought I'd check in with work before it's too late. I'll see you later?"

"Oh, okay," I nodded. I was confused . . . and maybe even a little hurt. Why didn't Raiden want to spend time with us?

Then I shook my head, chastising myself for thinking like that. Raiden had given up a whole day of work just to make sure I wouldn't worry about Cam when I went to work. I couldn't expect him to abandon his work completely for us. It was unfair of me to want him to stay.

"We'll see you later, then," I said and Raiden nodded quickly before walking off towards the front door.

"Ow!" I complained loudly when Cam pinched my side. I turned to glare at her. "What was that for?"

"Go stop him!" Cam hissed, scowling right back with real annoyance in her eyes.

"What? Why?"

"Ugh! I swear sometimes you adults are even more clueless than us kids!"

I waited for her to explain, and she rolled her eyes at me. Cheeky.

"Daddy! Didn't you see the look in his eyes?"

"I did. He looked sad. Was it because of me?"

"It was because of both of us, Daddy. In school, I had a friend. Daisy. We talked every day. She had another friend, James. They were neighbors too, so they were best friends. Anyway, Daisy and I would talk every day, but the moment James came into class, Daisy would start talking to him and completely forget me."

I didn't know what Cam's story had to do with our situation, and I was about to say the same to her when it clicked. *Oh.*

"You think that's the way Raiden felt?"

Cam nodded, biting her lower lip as her eyes started to water. "I did the same thing to him that Daisy did to me. I forgot all about him when you came home. He probably feels like I did, like he isn't a part of this, of us. You need to stop him before he leaves, Daddy. We can't let him go a second time."

I nodded because she was right. She was so right. About us making Raiden feel like he wasn't a part of us, and about not letting him go for a second time.

Cam waved at me to go, and I did. I raced out of the living room, hoping against hope that he'd still be in the foyer, but he wasn't.

"Fuck!" I cursed softly as I grabbed my keys from the bowl I'd dropped them in, ready to chase him all the way to his place if that was what it took.

Thankfully, though, I wouldn't need to leave Cam behind because there Raiden was, sitting in his car with his head resting on the steering wheel. He looked up when I walked out of the door, his eyes widening when he spotted me.

I waved at him, gesturing for him to step out of the car. He looked hesitant, but after a moment, he seemed to take a deep breath before opening the car door and stepping out. He closed it behind him but didn't come closer. Instead, he leaned against the car and watched me walk over.

I didn't beat around the bush. Instead, I asked him, "Why were you really leaving, Raiden? It wasn't because of work." I spoke in past tense because I wanted him to know there was no way he was leaving now, no way I was letting him leave.

"It was nothing."

"Raiden."

Raiden sighed, his eyes meeting mine before sliding away. But that one glance had been enough for me to see the turmoil in his gaze. Sadness. Pain. Confusion. Yearning.

"I . . . this morning, I felt like . . . like we were a unit. You, me, and Cam. I felt like we were a . . . family. And then, after you left, Cam and I spent the day together and it was perfect. And then you came back from work, and I realized I was just a stand-in for you. She doesn't need me in her family. She only needs you."

"And what about me? What about what I need?" I asked him, my voice soft. I wanted to correct him, wanted to tell him that Cam cared for him more than he knew. That it was because of her insistence that I'd taken a chance that day.

Raiden laughed, a broken, bitter laugh that pierced my heart worse than any words could've. "But you don't need me either, do you? Hell, you're not even sure if you're attracted to me."

He looked up at me then, his gray eyes stormy and full of a million different emotions. "I thought I finally had it, you know. I thought that after two thousand years of waiting, and waiting, and more fucking waiting, I had the family I'd always wanted.

"But then you came in, and Cam was hugging you and I realized . . . I realized I didn't fit in. The two of you, you're a family. And I don't fit in." Raiden shook his head, the devastated look in his eyes breaking my heart. It was even worse than the look he'd given me when I'd said no that first day. And I couldn't bear it.

"I . . . I'll go. You probably want to hang out with Cam, and yeah." Raiden nodded to himself, but before he could turn around, I closed the distance between us and wrapped my arms around him.

He froze in my arms, then tried to pull away, but I wouldn't let him. He was not allowed to pull away from me. From us.

I leaned closer to him and pressed a firm kiss in the middle of his forehead. Raiden's breath caught, his eyes flickering with surprise. In the past few weeks, Raiden had kissed me many times. On my cheeks, my temples, my forehead. I'd never reciprocated. Until now.

Raiden

William kissed me. My forehead tingled where his lips had been a moment ago, and I took a shuddering breath as I tried to wrap my head around what had just happened.

I wasn't sure where all those feelings, all those insecurities had come from, but I felt hollowed out. Empty. At least, I had, until William had pulled me closer and kissed me.

"You kissed me," I whispered softly, and William smiled. Then he kissed the spot right between my brows.

My knees almost buckled at the feel of his warm lips on my skin, and my hands came up to clutch his sides.

"Raiden, do you know why I messaged you that day?"

I knew without asking what day he was talking about. The day he'd given me a chance. The day he'd said he wanted to try. I shook my head in answer and he smiled. He placed a palm against my cheek, and I sank into the warmth of his skin.

"It was because Cam told me I should. She told me I was being stupid, called Raphael so he could tell me I was being stupid, and they both told me I needed to give you a chance."

Hearing those words made me happy but they also hurt. His words meant that Cam wanted me in her life, but they also made me wonder: did he? Had he just asked me to come back because his daughter had wanted him to?

"I can see what you're thinking, you know. I didn't message you that day just because Cam wanted me to. I did it because . . . because I realized that the real reason I'd hesitated was that I was still not over Veronica. I loved Cam's mom, and

I think I still do. But that doesn't mean I don't want you in my life. The last few weeks have been wonderful, and I want you to be a part of us, Raiden. Please don't leave us."

I searched William's eyes, and all I could see was honesty. He meant every word of what he'd said. They wanted me here. Wanted me to be a part of their family.

I took a deep breath, closed my eyes, and hoped with all my heart that it wouldn't get broken.

I looked at William, at his green eyes and the fierce sincerity in them, and nodded. "I don't want to leave either."

"Good. Now, let's go in before Cam starts freaking out."

The moment I stepped inside the front door, Camille slammed into me, her arms wrapping tightly around me, Snuffles nipping at our feet as he hopped around excitedly.

I swallowed the lump in my throat as I loosened Cam's arms just enough so I could pull her up and into my arms. She placed her hands on my cheeks, meeting my eyes. Her bright blue eyes were watery, and her chin wobbled as she looked at me.

"I'm so sorry, DD. I wasn't a very good friend to you. I didn't mean to abandon you like that."

"Oh sweetie, it's okay. No tears, yeah?"

Cam hastily wiped her eyes and shook her head. "Nope. No tears anywhere, DD."

I smiled at her and kissed her nose, making her giggle. William approached once he'd shut the front door and wrapped his arms around both of us, and a quiet relief overwhelmed me. Could this really be happening?

"Do you know why I call you DD?" Cam asked, her eyes flashing like she'd just made a decision.

"You refused to tell us what it meant, remember?" William piped up, a grin on his face as he looked between us.

Cam shot him a glance before turning back to me. She squeezed my cheeks between her palms, making me chuckle.

"I didn't plan on telling you what it meant so soon. But I think now is the perfect time to say it." She took a deep breath, glanced at William one last time, before turning back to me.

"DD means Dragon Dad," Cam said softly, and I froze. All this time . . . "You are a part of this family, DD. You're not an outsider. You're a part of us. You take care of me just like Daddy does. You know what to do to cheer me or Daddy up. You take care of Daddy too. You're a part of us, DD."

This time, it was my eyes that watered, but I couldn't be bothered to give a damn about it. William's arms tightened around us, and I glanced at him, wondering if he didn't want Cam to be thinking of me as her . . . as her father. But no, William had a smile on his face, a soft look in his eyes as he met mine. And right there, with William's—with our daughter in my arms and with my mate beside me, I finally felt like I was home. Like I was complete.

Six

William

"Will you go somewhere with me?" I asked Raiden between sips of coffee while gazing out the window to avoid looking at him. It had been a few weeks since I'd gone back to work, but I'd taken today off because it was Cam's first day back at school, and I'd known I'd just get on Avery's nerves if I went in.

Raiden, showing me yet again what a wonderful and kind man he was, had come over an hour before I was supposed to drop Cam to school, and we'd done it together before coming back to my place. The moment we'd stepped into the house, I'd turned right around and hugged Raiden, and he'd held me while I'd gathered my strength, assuring me again and again that Cam would be okay.

We may not have gotten around to getting physical yet, but I felt it deep in my soul . . . I was falling for Raiden, for his steady, comforting presence, for the way he took care of me. I was falling in love with him, and it didn't scare me in the least.

But before I went any further, before I removed that last barrier between us, I needed to do something. I needed to visit someone and assure her that no matter what, she'd always be my first love.

"Of course. Where do you want to go?"

"The Silent Creek Cemetery."

The realization was instant on Raiden's face, his mouth forming a small O before he nodded, a strand of his white-blond hair flopping over his forehead.

I dumped my mug into the sink and walked over to him. I pushed the stray strand of hair off his forehead as I looked into his eyes. "Would you rather I go alone?" I asked. I wanted to take him with me, wanted Veronica to meet the man I was falling for, and wanted Raiden to meet the woman I'd loved for so long. But if the idea made Raiden uncomfortable, I wouldn't force him.

"Oh no, of course not. I'd like to come with you."

I nodded and leaned forward, resting my forehead against his, marveling at how easy it was to be close to him. Was I hesitating for no good reason? I knew the idea of being close to Raiden, of being intimate with him, didn't make me want to freak out, so why hadn't I kissed him yet?

I knew he wouldn't be the one to make the first move, knew he was ready to wait for months if that was what it took. Hell, we'd already been together for almost three months, if you could call what we were doing dating. But that wasn't fair. We were dating. After all, not all romantic relationships included sex. Having sex wasn't the be-all and end-all of relationships.

"You're so good to me, Ray. Thank you for being so patient. I . . . you don't know how much it means to me, everything you've done for me. You make me feel . . . treasured. Loved. And I . . . I'm falling for you."

Raiden's warm breath ghosted over my lips. He was so close. I could feel the heat radiating from his taut body. It wouldn't take much to press my mouth to his. But before that . . . "I want to say goodbye to Veronica. I want you to meet her, stupid as it sounds, and I want to tell her that I'm happy. I guess, in a way, I want her approval? No, not approval. I want her blessings before I can . . . before I can let myself be with you completely. I know it sounds—"

"It sounds absolutely perfect, and I would like nothing more than to get Veronica's blessings. I'd like to meet her and assure her that I'll take care of you and Cam," Raiden said, no hint of mockery in his voice, just plain acceptance and sincerity. And why had I expected anything different from him?

"Thank you," I said, my voice barely more than a choked off whisper.

Raiden's warm palm rubbed my back in a slow, soothing motion, our eyes still locked together. I could see nothing but adoration and care and protection in his eyes, all of it directed at me. And it made me feel strong, stronger than I remembered feeling in a long time.

Ever since Veronica died, I'd felt lost. Incomplete. Adrift. And when Cam got sick? Then everything had turned worse, and I'd been so terrified. And so damn alone. But now, in Raiden's arms, for the first time in what felt like eons, I felt safe. At ease. Happy.

I pulled away with a sigh, reluctant to let go of that cozy feeling but knowing I needed to do this. I needed to turn the page and start a new chapter of my life with Raiden. But before that, I needed to say goodbye to Veronica one last time.

"Alright. I'm ready. Let's go."

Raiden

The Silent Creek Cemetery was beautiful. I hadn't had much reason to visit a cemetery in a long, long time, but I remembered the serene atmosphere of the place. It didn't matter what cemetery it was, they all felt similar.

The weather today was that perfect balance between cool and warm, where one wouldn't mind going on a long walk just to enjoy the pleasantness of it. I'd made sure of it. While most days my magic affected the weather without input from me, today I'd consciously worked to make the day as balmy as I could, so this task would be just a bit easier for William.

A light breeze blew through the trees, making leaves and dry flowers flutter around. It made the cemetery feel like a cheerful, happy place. Yes, the dead were buried here, but it was still a joyful place. A place where the dead were at peace. I could sense it in the air, the hundreds of souls who had found peace here before drifting off to the next phase of life.

William held my hand tightly as we walked through the grass, following a path that he seemed to know by heart. He hadn't let go of my hand since we got out of the car, and it warmed my heart that he knew he could depend on me like this.

I squeezed his hand in support when he slowed, and he squeezed back as we finally came to a stop in front of a beautiful black marble tombstone. The grave was surrounded by wildflower bushes, giving it a cheerful look. It was clear William—and maybe even Camille—had gone to great lengths to make Veronica's final resting place a pleasant one.

Veronica Hawthorne.

Beloved Wife And Mother.

Chase your stars, fool. Life is short.

I smiled at the quote. From everything Will and Cam had told me about Veronica, she had been a bright, kind woman who'd loved her family dearly. When William asked me to come here with him, I hadn't just said yes for his sake. I'd wanted to visit her too, to assure her that I'd take good care of her family.

William dropped my hand and walked closer to the grave, falling to his knees and taking a seat in the grass near the stone. I was debating if he would prefer to have some privacy or not, but before I could ask, he motioned me over by patting the space beside him. I didn't waste a moment as I sat down, mirroring his position so I was facing the tombstone.

"Hey V," William said softly, brushing away the dry flowers that scattered across the stone. "I haven't been here in a while, huh? I'm so sorry about that. With everything that happened with Cam . . . you know what? I don't have an excuse. I was avoiding coming here because I didn't know how to tell you this, or what you'd think of me for it."

William glanced up at me, his bright green eyes troubled and filled with a sadness I never wanted to see on his face. He looked his age in this moment, and I hated it. I gave him a reassuring smile and nodded. He returned my smile and turned back to face the stone.

"I wanted to tell you about Raiden, V. I . . . I didn't expect this to happen. Any of this. But . . . but I'm falling in love with Raiden, and I need your blessings, sweetheart. I need you to know that I'll always love you, that you'll always be my first love and Cam's mom. I'm not . . . I'm not replacing you. I'm just giving myself the permission to love again, and I hope you'll be happy for me. For us."

When it didn't look like William had anything more to say, I took a deep breath and started speaking. "Hello, Veronica. If you've been watching over your family, you know who I am. I want you to know that I'll treasure your family the way they deserve to be treasured. I'll keep them safe and love them with all I am. I do not mean to, or hope to, replace you. I just want to be a part of your family, to love them and be loved by them in return."

I placed my palm on the gravestone and smiled at the emotions that filled me. Veronica wasn't in this world, in this realm, anymore, but wherever she was, she was happy and safe. She was linked to this place, though, just like she was linked to William and Cam, and I could sense an echo of what she felt.

"She's happy for you, Will," I said softly, and William's eyes shot to mine, full of questions.

I offered him my palm, and he took my hand, his warm fingers enveloping mine. I closed my eyes and let myself be a conduit between them, letting William feel what I'd felt.

I opened my eyes to find him watching me, a soft smile on his face. "She's happy. Safe. Content. Relieved."

"I think . . ." I started but faltered because I was unsure if William would appreciate what I wanted to say. When he gave me an encouraging nod, I continued, "I think she's relieved you're not alone anymore."

William smiled then, a bright, wide smile that made butterflies wreak havoc in my chest. "I think you're right."

And then William did something completely unexpected. He leaned forward and pressed his mouth to mine. It was a simple press of lips against lips and ended within seconds, but it was everything.

And when a strong wind blew wildflowers over us as we parted? We knew we had all the blessings we needed.

Seven

William

By the time we arrived at home, all my doubts were gone. I hadn't had many to begin with, but the biggest one had disappeared the moment Raiden had shown me what he could sense from Veronica. She was okay with this, with me moving on. And why had I ever doubted it in the first place? Veronica was one of the most selfless people I knew, and I knew she would've pulled my ear and reprimanded me if she knew I'd been avoiding my own happiness because I thought she would want me to.

If the situation were reversed, I'd have wanted her to move on too. So why did I ever think she wouldn't want the same for me?

A bottle of water appeared before me, uncapped, and I took it gratefully. Drinking a big gulp, I looked at Raiden. He was a gorgeous man, and I realized that I hadn't told him that enough. In my attempt to keep from moving on, I'd held back so much from him when he'd just kept on giving and giving. How could I have been so selfish?

The words he'd said to me in the driveway still echoed in my head, his broken, sad voice as he'd said that he didn't think I was even attracted to him. Had I really been so caught up in my own shit that I'd misled Raiden so completely? That I'd made him feel like I felt nothing for him?

I went back over all the time we'd spent together in the past few months, all the hours spent in each other's company, and I almost swore out loud when I realized what an idiot I'd been.

In almost three months, Raiden had become an inseparable part of our family. He fit in with us perfectly, and he'd become a part of our routine with barely any problems. But in having him become a part of our family, I'd forgotten something that was just as important. Us. The two of us. We'd been "dating" for almost three months, yet we hadn't been on a single actual date.

I shook my head, incredulous at my own stupidity. No wonder Raiden thought I wasn't interested in him. I'd done nothing to show him otherwise. First, I'd rejected him, and then I'd basically treated him like I would a friend. He was a saint to have stayed with me after all I've put him through. But that changed now.

"Hey Raiden," I said and he looked up at me from where he was grabbing a bottle of water for himself. I walked over to him, took the bottle of water from his hand, and placed it on the counter. Now that I'd realized how much of an asshole I'd been, I needed to rectify it immediately. I needed Raiden to know that I cared about him, that I wanted him.

I slid closer, placing my palms on either side of him so he was trapped against the refrigerator. He swallowed hard, his Adam's apple bobbing as his eyes met mine.

"William?" His voice was soft, breathy.

I leaned in, our noses almost touching as I looked into his gray eyes. They were lighter today, bright with an inner glow.

I breathed in the scent of his light cologne and the fainter scent of rainstorms that seemed to be all him. It was a heady mix, and my patience ran thin as I finally, finally pressed my mouth to his.

Our lips slotted together perfectly, as if they'd been made for each other. His hands came up my back, gripping onto the tops of my shoulders as he pressed our bodies together. It was so different from kissing a woman. Soft curves were replaced by hard planes, smooth cheeks by scruffy ones. His moans were deeper, reaching all the way into my soul. It was different, yes, but no less consuming.

I lost myself to it, to the feel of his warm lips around mine, my tongue in his mouth, tasting, exploring, marking. He was mine, and I was his, and nothing had felt this perfect before.

When breathing became a necessity, I came up for air, albeit reluctantly, but I pulled him with me, wrapping my arms around him as I rested my forehead against his. His eyes were dark as they met mine, the gray swirling around as he watched me, his lips red and swollen and so damn kissable. His breathing seemed to be completely even, but his eyes told me he was just as affected by the kiss as I was.

I jumped as a loud crack of thunder sounded above us, and Raiden's arms tightened around me. He gave me a sheepish smile. "Sorry. My magic got a bit . . . excited."

I chuckled, shaking my head and pressing another soft kiss to his lips. My phone pinged in my pocket, reminding me I needed to pick up Cam in half an hour.

"What do you say we go pick Cam up and then have some late lunch someplace to celebrate her first day back at school?"

Raiden blinked a few times, his brows crinkling adorably as he tried to make sense of my words. When it finally clicked, he nodded. "Oh yes, that sounds wonderful."

"Great. But before that, I need to kiss you again." And so I did.

Camille

I spotted them the moment I stepped out of the school gates. A grin spread across my lips when I saw both Dad and DD waiting by Dad's car, standing close to each other. Closer than I'd ever seen them.

Hmmm . . .

"You're both here!" I stepped up to them, smiling widely. I hugged DD first because I still felt bad about the other day and then hugged my dad.

"Yeah, we thought we could go out for lunch, all three of us. How does that sound?" Dad asked and I couldn't stop grinning.

"It sounds perfect!" I climbed into the backseat and waited impatiently for them to get in the car.

"Can we go to One Stop and get lunch from Mama's Kitchen? And maybe dessert from Crystal's Bakery?" I popped the questions as soon as they were both inside and Dad chuckled.

"Sure, sweetie. But first, tell us how your day was."

And so I did. I told them all about my first day, and they listened to every word, chipping in every once in a while with comments that assured me they were really listening.

When we'd almost reached TOSS—who has the time to say The One Stop Shops again and again?—I asked them, "So what did you guys do today?"

DD glanced at Dad with a raised brow, and Dad smiled softly. He met my eyes in the rearview mirror and placed his hand on top of DD's. "We visited your mom and asked for her blessings for this new family of ours."

That was why they looked so cozy! Dad finally removed the last wall that had been standing between him and DD. I didn't remember my mom since I'd only been three years old when she died, but I knew she was a kind, sweet woman. And I knew she'd be delighted to see us all happy now.

"That deserves a chocolate chip dessert," I told them, making them both laugh as I grinned and leaned back in my seat. Dad had finally accepted DD with his whole heart. Next step: get the two of them to go out on a date. Without me.

By the time we got seated in the Food Court at TOSS, I'd decided what I wanted to eat. DD went to place our order at Mama's Kitchen, making me smile because I knew he didn't like talking to strangers and was doing it just for me, and I turned to face Dad.

"You need to take him out on a date, Daddy." I'd expected Dad to chuckle or roll his eyes, but instead, he nodded as if he'd been thinking the same thing.

"Yeah, I do. I realized today that I haven't done much to show him how much he means to me, and I need to change that. I'm working on it, sweetie, I promise."

Well, that was all I needed to hear. Except . . . "I have a few ideas, if you need any."

He did roll his eyes this time. "I don't need your ideas, biscuit. I'm not so far out of the game that I need dating advice from my daughter."

I shrugged, though I couldn't stop myself from grinning. I hadn't seen this version of Dad in a long time. Carefree, smiling . . . happy. When I was younger, I would catch him with tears in his eyes. Whenever I would ask, he would tell me a story about mom that he'd suddenly remembered. I imagined his sadness like a garden, no flowers, only weeds, wild and thick, then everything had just gotten worse when I became sick.

I shook off the unhappy thoughts. I needed to remember that was in the past. We had DD now, and Dad was finally happy again, which made me happy. His garden was full of the prettiest flowers now, and it was all thanks to DD.

DD returned to the table then, telling us our order would be ready in ten minutes. Dad and DD chatted about work, so I ignored them and did something I enjoyed, people watching.

I caught DD waving at someone from the corner of my eye and looked up to find him whispering something to dad, who then looked at someone behind me.

Curious, I turned around and excitement crackled through my stomach when I recognized the man. Before my dads could stop me, I was out of my chair and racing over to him.

"Cam!" Dad called behind me, but I ignored him as I reached the big man whom I'd met only once before but knew I could trust.

"Mr. Magician's friend! Hi! Where's your bird?"

Mr. Magician's friend, whose name was Cassian if I remembered correctly, chuckled. "She's back home. Couldn't bring her here, right? Oh, by the way, this is Gustave. You can call him Gus if you want. He's my boyfriend."

"Oooh, are you magic boyfriends? Mates like Mr. Magician and Jai?" I needed to start calling Raphael by his name, but Mr. Magician sounded like a superhero name, and he was my superhero. He'd saved my life.

"Yep, exactly like that," Cassian answered, and I remembered I could tell him about DD. Finally! Someone I didn't have to hide the truth from.

"Awesome! My daddy has a mate too! He's a dragon, but it's supposed to be a secret, so don't tell anyone." I pressed my finger to my lips for added effect, and Gus chuckled just as Daddy finally reached us. What had taken him so long?

"Your daughter is really bad at keeping secrets, William," Cassian said with a laugh, and Dad shook his head before glaring at me, though his lips twitched, which meant I wasn't in trouble.

"Nah, she just knows she can tell you guys because Raiden told her she could," Dad explained, pointing at DD who was still sitting at our table. Was he protecting our food or just not up to being social?

He waved at us, a small smile on his face, and I realized it was the second option.

The other man, Cassian's mate, smiled brightly. He was a tiny guy, especially in comparison to Cassian's huge size, with longish black hair and beautiful purple eyes that I'd never seen before. Something told me he wasn't human. I wondered what he was, but it seemed like a rude question to ask.

"Hey Cassian, tell Raphael I want to see him again sometime? I want to meet Neya and see Padfoot and Jai again too. And your bird. Her name is April, right?"

Cassian nodded, his yellow-orange eyes sparkling brightly as he said, "I'll let Raph know that Princess Camille has demanded an audience with him."

I giggled before giving him a quick hug. Hugging Cassian was like hugging a fireplace—with all the coziness and none of the burn injuries, of course.

Then, I walked over and hugged Gus, freezing immediately when I realized how cold he was. "You're so cold! Are you okay?"

"I am, sweetheart. Don't worry about me."

Before I could ask him the question that was begging to jump out of my mouth, Dad was steering me back toward our table, telling the two men that we'd see them again soon.

"What is Gus?" I asked DD as soon as I reached our table, making both dads chuckle.

"Would you like to make a guess?" DD asked and I grinned.

"What do I get if I guess right?"

"A big cone of chocolate chip ice cream, all yours."

"Deal!" I already had an idea, between his pale, cold skin and his strangely beautiful eyes, but I still made a show of thinking it over.

"Oh, I know!" I exclaimed before biting my tongue when I realized how loud I'd been.

"Sorry," I whispered and Dad shook his head as he pushed my burger closer to me.

"Eat before it gets cold."

I nodded, took a big bite, and promptly realized I couldn't answer DD now. I chewed as fast as I could, swallowed, and gasped out, "He's a vampire." All the signs pointed to that, except for the fact that Gus was so . . . smiley when every vampire on TV or in books was always angry or grumpy.

DD grinned at me before grabbing a tissue and wiping my chin with it. I looked down and spotted the sauce covered tissue. *Oops.*

"Correct answer!" DD declared and I wiggled in my seat.

Chocolate chip ice cream! Yes!

Eight

William

"I'll be fine," Camille insisted and then promptly sneezed again.

"But you're not fine." I barely kept the frustration out of my voice. Yes, I'd been excited about finally taking Raiden out on a date. But that didn't mean that I was ready to leave Camille alone when she was sick.

"I'm not alone, Dad. Rose will be here with me. I want you to go, please," Camille said, not budging at all. Then, before I could say another word, she turned to Raiden. "DD, didn't you say I wouldn't get sick now that I'm part of your hoard?"

Now that she mentioned it, I remembered Raiden telling us that. I glanced up at him and found him blushing as he opened his mouth, though no words came out. He seemed to struggle for a minute more. Finally, he took a deep breath, shooting me a glance before turning to Camille.

"That is true, Cam. But even though I consider you a part of my hoard, the bond isn't complete yet. I can't just go around claiming humans as a part of my hoard, you know? Therefore, there are some restrictions."

"Restrictions? Like what?" Camille sniffed, wiping her nose with the tissue she had balled up in her hands. Snuffles sniffed at the tissues and Cam pulled her hand away, chastising him.

"Well, for one, we need to complete the bond between us. Nothing major, you just need to accept that you are a part of my hoard and that I am a part of yours. For dragons, their hoard is a mix of their most treasured possessions and their family. I do consider both of you my family already, but before I can completely bond with you Camille, I need to . . ." Raiden's blush darkened even further. He seemed to fortify himself by taking another deep breath. "I need to complete my bond with your father."

Camille stared at him, just like I did, before we both seemed to come to the same realization at the exact same moment. While red spread across my cheeks, Camille grinned wickedly, her eyes shooting between us.

"Oh! You mean you need to do the nasty with my dad before we can be a part of your hoard!"

My face had never been as red as it was right now, but Raiden looked even worse off than me. He was looking anywhere but at us, and my heart went out to him. He looked so embarrassed, and yet he had told Camille everything without holding back. I walked over to him and wrapped my arm around his waist, pulling him into my side before giving Camille a mock glare.

"Alright Missy, if you are done embarrassing my boyfriend, we're going to get going. Promise me you will call me if you feel any worse." I didn't miss the way Raiden jerked when I called him my boyfriend, but I just ignored it for the moment, though I knew I would be mentioning it later. I wanted to make sure there were no doubts between us, that Raiden knew exactly how much he meant to me.

The smile on Camille's face flickered for a moment, and I wondered if she was really sure about letting me go, but before I could grab onto the expression, she shook her head and smiled at us.

"Go! I will be fine. Have fun!" She blew kisses at us and Raiden blew some back before I led him out of the house.

Now that we were finally headed out, the butterflies started fluttering in my stomach, and I wondered if Raiden would enjoy what I had planned for us. There wasn't a lot to do in Mistvale, but I hoped this would be something he would enjoy.

When we reached my car, I opened the passenger door for Raiden without thought, and he smiled softly before getting inside. I walked around to the driver's side and got in, smiling back at him as I settled into my seat.

"Are we really going on a date?" Raiden asked, his voice as soft and sweet as usual.

"Yeah, we are. I wanted to spend some time with you. Just the two of us." I admitted, wiping my palms on my thighs.

Raiden's smile brightened a notch, and I felt some of the tension ease out of me as I started the car. I hoped he would enjoy where I was taking him. Back when Veronica had been alive, I'd enjoyed boating a lot. Though she had never accompanied me since she was afraid of larger bodies of water, she had never stopped me from taking a day off to go fishing or spending weekends on the lake. I didn't plan on fishing today, but I did plan on taking Raiden for a boat ride.

I drove through the town to the docks, and we discussed everything from Camille's school to the movies we wanted to see. As we talked, I realized Raiden had spent barely any time away from the two of us in the past few weeks. More times than I could count, Raiden had crashed in the guestroom. And other days, he would leave after dinner but be right back the next day after work. I didn't mention it though because I didn't want him to stop coming over. Raiden had brightened up my and Camille's life, and I never wanted him to leave. But that was too soon, wasn't it? To ask him to move in with me? When I had just kissed him for the first time. Yeah, it was definitely too soon.

"The docks?" Raiden had a puzzled look on his face as he turned this way and that in his seat. I parked the car, grateful that there didn't seem to be many people in the area.

"Yeah, I thought we could go boating? Unless you're afraid of being out on the water too." Holy shit, what if he was? I should've asked him before I brought us here.

"Boating sounds wonderful! What did you mean about me being scared of water, too? Is Camille scared of it?"

"No, actually, Veronica was—" I stopped speaking. I shouldn't be talking about my dead wife on my date, right?

A warm hand wrapped around my chin, and Raiden turned my face to his. I looked into his light-gray eyes, swirling captivatingly like they always did.

"William, please don't do that. I understand Veronica was a big part of your life. You love her. You have a beautiful daughter with her. Please don't mince your words for me. This relationship . . . it isn't just between the two of us. It never was. It's you and me, yes, but Camille and Veronica are just as much a part of it. And I accept that. Please feel free to talk about her all you want. I'd love to hear about her whenever you wish to share. She loved you, William. How could I ever think anything but the best of her?"

There was a big lump in my throat that I just couldn't get rid of. I wanted to tell him how much his words meant to me.

He'd said I love Veronica. Present tense. And he was right. I did love her. I'd always love her. But I was starting to realize that my heart was capable of loving more than one person. I may have just kissed Raiden, but I knew without a doubt that I was in love with him.

Yes, he was a man, but he was also the most sweet, kind, and gorgeous person I'd ever met. I'd fallen for Veronica in high school, so maybe if I hadn't, I would've discovered that I was bisexual, but that didn't matter. I wouldn't change a thing. I love Veronica and I love Raiden. But I couldn't tell him that yet. Too soon. It was too damn soon.

"Let's go find ourselves a boat." I pressed a soft kiss to his temple, my *thank you* for everything he'd said.

The "find ourselves a boat" part had been just a way to get us moving, since I'd already booked one. It was a cute little thing with big oars and just enough space for the two of us. I'd also paid them extra to pack us a picnic, and I nodded approvingly when I spotted the cooler tucked under the bench.

"Oh, this is such a cute boat." Raiden smiled at me, and I grinned back as I waved at him to take a seated. I sat across from him, resting my hands on the oars, letting my fingers find the perfect grip while Raiden situated himself. "This was a really great idea, William. And the weather's perfect for it too."

I chuckled at the cheeky remark. "All thanks to you, of course."

"Consider it my contribution to our date." Raiden's shoulders dropped, and a peaceful look slid onto his face. An elated feeling overtook me in that moment, and I started to row.

"Tell me more about your magic," I requested, watching Raiden dipped his fingers into the water as he took in our surroundings. I followed his gaze, taking in the Silent Creek Park on one side and the gently moving water on the other. I knew somewhere to our right, hidden behind a veil of magic, was Ravenshire, the island that had been home to Raphael and Cassian at one time. Raphael had told me—well, he'd told Camille, and I'd been close enough to listen in—about the island, about the bigoted assholes who lived there. But he'd also told us how it was one of the most beautiful places in the world. It was a shame the people—the mages—that lived there had ruined the place.

"What would you like to know?" Raiden pulled his hand back to his lap, and it took me a second to remember what I'd asked him.

"Just . . . how it works, what you can do, stuff like that. Only if you want to, of course. I understand if there are things you can't tell me."

Raiden frowned, tilting his head as he looked at me. His white-blond hair glinted in the warm sunlight, making him appear almost angelic. I was tempted to call him angel, but Camille had vetoed it because Jai called Raphael that, and in Camille's words, *My dad will not be a copycat!*

"Why wouldn't I tell you?" He seemed honestly stumped.

"Um, you know, there might be secret dragon things you're not allowed to tell anyone."

Raiden smiled softly, though it seemed to be tinged by something else, something I couldn't quite place. Sadness?

"William . . . there's nothing, absolutely nothing, about myself that I wouldn't share with you. You're my mate. I know the term and its implications are unfamiliar to you, but a mate is any magical creature's most treasured. Hell, if a human is lucky enough to find their fated mate, they would do anything for them too."

"Humans? You mean like Jai would do anything for Raphael?" Raiden had met Jai and Raphael a few times now, and we'd all become good friends in the past few weeks.

"Yes, but also humans who are mated to other humans. Most magical creatures are able to sense their mates, but every living, thinking being has a fated mate. Humans don't always find theirs, but there are some who are lucky enough to."

Oh, wow. I hadn't known that. If that was true, Veronica could've been . . . but no, Raiden had also said a person can have only one fated mate, which meant she hadn't been mine . . .

As if he'd read my mind, Raiden smiled softly at me, resting his palm on my knee. "That isn't to say that you can't love someone you aren't fated to, William. A lot of times, even magical creatures give up on ever finding their fated one and instead settle with someone they've created a bond with."

"Did you?" I placed my hand atop his and startled as I realized I'd stopped rowing. But looking around, it seemed like the perfect place to take a break and just . . . talk.

"Did I what?"

"Give up on finding your fated one? Finding me?"

Raiden sighed, his eyes flickering as he looked around, gathering his thoughts. "Yes, and no. Two thousand years is a long time to spend alone, William. I don't remember my brood-mother or my broodmates. My first clear memories are of roaming through mountains, finding a cave, keeping myself fed. I remember a lot, but most of all, I remember the loneliness.

"I'd been alone, utterly alone, for a long time before I stumbled across a small village of humans. I made the mistake of visiting them in my true form the very first time, but once I realized they feared me, I used my magic to change my appearance to look more like them. Slowly, I learned their language and became a part of human society. I had . . . relations, encounters really, which were attempts at finding a mate or just someone to keep the loneliness at bay."

Raiden swallowed, his eyes a shade darker than they'd been. The sky, a mirror of his eyes as always, turned darker too, clouds gathering to make it seem like it was evening already when it was barely noon. He shook his head, as if shaking off the dark clouds.

"Anyway, a few hundred years ago, I decided I'd had enough of searching, enough of hoping, and I turned back into the hermit I'd been, though I couldn't go back to living as a dragon in this modern world. And then, just when I'd resigned myself to spending another thousand years alone, I stepped into a stranger's house for a meeting . . . and found you." He smiled then, a bright smile that was so full of joy I looked up at the sky, half-expecting the clouds to just vanish and shower us with sunlight. Instead, the barest of rays peeked through the clouds, though they did seem to be shifting.

"You said you knew I was your mate because of my scent, right?"

Raiden nodded, and I thought back to the day we'd first met.

"But it wasn't when we first met, was it? You were . . . different after I . . ."

"After you returned from your shower, yes." Raiden wrinkled his nose and smiled. "The cologne you'd been wearing was bothering my nose."

My mouth fell open. "That's why you brought me that cologne?" I'd been confused when he'd gifted me with cologne of all things, but I'd shrugged it off as one of his dragon-quirks.

Raiden grinned. "Maybe?"

I shook my head as I pulled the cooler out from under his bench. "Okay, tell me more. What else can you do with your magic other than change the weather and your own form?"

Raiden

"Seriously? You can change what someone else looks like?" William's voice was full of disbelief, and I couldn't fault him for doubting me. It was a pretty strange power, and I wasn't sure why I had it. In all my time in this world, I'd encountered only one other dragon, and they hadn't had the power at all. I had a feeling Fate had a role in it, just like she did in everything else.

"I can't change their appearance completely. But individual features, yes."

"So, you mean you could turn my eyes blue to match Camille's?"

"I could, but I won't."

"Why not?"

"Because, I find your green eyes rather mesmerizing, and I would prefer they stay the same."

Pink spread across William's scruffy cheeks, and it made me smile. But I didn't want him to feel too embarrassed, so I continued, "I haven't used that power much, but at one time I made fortunes as a plastic surgeon. Burn victims, people who wanted to increase or decrease the size of their body parts, I helped them. Of course, this was before doctors actually learned how to do the same. By then, I'd moved on because the last thing I needed was for people to question my methods and wonder how I did what I did."

William shook his head and then proceeded to ask me another hundred questions. At this moment, I could see clearly how similar he and Camille were. They had the same curiosity about everything, and I loved it. I loved them. Between bites of sandwich and sips of beer, I answered all of William's questions, delighting in the way he showed an interest in my past and me.

When he had called me his boyfriend, I had been surprised. I'd had a few bedmates over the years, but I'd never had a boyfriend. I hadn't been able to bring myself to form an emotional relationship with someone when I knew my mate was somewhere out there. And now that I had met William, I was glad I had resisted. William was everything I could have ever wanted in a boyfriend, in a mate, and I was glad I had waited for him.

When William had exhausted all his questions, I took the oars from him, turning us back in the direction we had come. William had been rowing on and off while we talked, and he'd come quite a ways. I smiled at him, loving the way the water's reflection sparkled in his green eyes. He was so beautiful. And all mine.

"At home . . . you called me your boyfriend," I murmured and William smiled at me, his eyes brightening even further.

"Well, you are, aren't you?"

"I am. And you're mine. My first."

William's brows furrowed, and he gave me a puzzled look. "Your first? First what?"

My cheeks warmed slightly at the admission, but I trudged on. "My first boyfriend."

"First boyfriend? But I thought . . . you said . . ."

I shook my head, clearing my throat. "I . . . bedded people, yes." My cheeks darkened, but I forced myself to continue, wanting William to know every part of me. "Men, women, people in between, but they meant nothing to me. I hoped to find someone, to find you, but when I didn't . . . I couldn't bring myself to form a relationship with them. I wanted to wait for my fated one to share those firsts with them. With you."

William smiled at that, his eyes warm and his cheeks slightly pink. But then he frowned, and a worried look passed over his face. "Are you disappointed with me, then? That I didn't wait for you?"

Even the thought of William not being just the way he was scared me. And not having Camille in our lives? I couldn't imagine that. I shook my head, making sure the oars were steady before stretching my hand out and grabbing William's. "Oh no, my sweet Will. I could never hold your past against you. I told you, Veronica was a part of your life, and I respect that. And, I cannot imagine our lives without Camille in it, so please don't think I have any problem with your past. You weren't to know about us, were you? Why would you wait?"

William nodded and blew out a soft breath. He gave me a rueful smile and squeezed my hand. "Sorry, I don't know why I freaked out there."

"It's alright, my dear." I leaned over carefully and pressed a soft kiss on his lips before pulling away. I took the oars back into my hands and began rowing.

William ducked his head, but I could hear the smile in his voice when he said, "Well, for what it's worth, you're my first boyfriend too."

And how I smiled.

By the time we reached the docks, the sun was dropping towards the West, and William looked even more gorgeous than he had before. His cheeks were flushed with warmth, his green eyes glittering with joy. Dressed in a soft, pale-blue T-shirt and dark jeans, he looked completely at ease and delightfully happy.

My heart burned with pride when I realized that smile was because of me, because of the time we had spent together.

As much as I wanted to go back home—to William's place, I corrected myself—and check on Camille, I didn't want our time together to end. Before I could ask William to stay for a bit longer, he turned to me and asked, "Would you like to grab coffee? As much as I want to go home, I don't want this day to end just yet." It was like he had read my mind, and I couldn't stop the grin that spread across my lips.

"Actually, can I take you somewhere?"

"Sure, where?" William stepped to the dock with the sure movements of a practiced boatman. He tied off the small skiff and offered me his hand.

I swallowed. It had been three months since I'd found William, and yet he'd never been to my house. It was probably because we tended to gather at his place, where Camille was most comfortable and had everything she needed, but I had a sudden urge to show William more of myself. After all, he was my mate. If he didn't know everything about me, who would?

"I was thinking . . . maybe we could go to my place?" I took his hand and held my breath as I waited for his response, wondering if he would say no. I need not have worried though, because a wide smile immediately spread across William's face, and he tugged me to dock.

"Yes! That would be wonderful." Before I could say another word, William handed me the keys to his car and started walking toward it. I hurried to catch up and raised a brow at him.

"You trust me with your car?" I asked, running my thumb over the fob.

William halted in step, and his eyes turned serious. "I trust you with my life, Raiden. More than that, I trust you with Camille's life."

My heart warmed, my whole body feeling as if it had just been doused in sunshine. I stepped up to him and wrapped my arms around his neck, pulling him closer to me. Closing my eyes, I pressed a soft kiss on his lips. I didn't mean for it to linger, but William pulled me closer and deepened the kiss, his lips tasting of beer and him. Sweet, sweet him. I moaned softly into his mouth, and his lips smiled against mine before he finally broke away. I rested my forehead against his and let out a happy sigh, my lips barely an inch away from his. "You say the sweetest things, my love."

I hadn't meant to call him "my love," but I wouldn't take it back. I did love him, even if he wasn't ready for it yet. And I wanted him to know. His eyes widened slightly, but he said nothing, just kept smiling at me, his bottomless green eyes full of joy.

Not wanting to, but knowing I should, I stepped away from him and opened the passenger door, moving aside with a gesture for him to slide in. He grinned at me as he obliged, and I couldn't resist leaning in for another kiss.

My home wasn't far from his, since we lived in the same neighborhood of old mansions and high-rise buildings. It made me wonder why we'd never crossed paths before, but Fate was strange that way. We drove through the town in a comfortable silence, soft music playing in the background. When we finally reached my door, I entered the security code and turned to smile at William.

"Welcome to my home."

Nine

William

Raiden's house was similar to mine in size and design. Built before my time, it was an imposing, and yet, it felt . . . safe. Like a place where I wouldn't need to worry about anything.

The floor plan was like my place too, and I wondered if the people who had built our houses were the same, or related. Which made me wonder . . .

"Hey, Ray?"

"Yeah?"

"How long have you lived here?" I asked, inspecting high ceilings and vast hardwood floors.

"Around twenty years, give or take. I do most of my work from home, and when I do go out, I change my appearance a bit since my employees know I've been their boss for the last twenty years, and I definitely don't look the age like this."

I chuckled because he was right. No way would someone believe this man was forty years old, much less two thousand. Twenty-five would be the most I'd be willing to accept him as, and even that was a stretch.

Raiden gave me the tour of his house, and it took me a moment to realize what was missing. There were no pictures on the walls, the mantles, or any of the shelves. Where my place was full of framed pictures of Cam, Veronica, and me—and a few recent ones with Raiden in them—Raiden's place was devoid of any memories. It was a beautiful place, but it wasn't home.

The last room Raiden led me to was his bedroom. I was about to make a joke about why this wasn't the first room we visited when he led me to a set of wooden doors.

Raiden opened them to reveal a . . . closet. Well, that was unexpected. And anticlimactic. But then Raiden walked in, his hand still wrapped around mine, and I followed.

My brows shot up when I realized there was another door behind the coat rack with a security code panel beside it.

"Are you taking me to Narnia?" I asked with a smirk. Living with a nine-year-old meant I knew all about the goat-legged man and the talking lion.

Raiden chuckled, entering the code with his left hand as he tightened the fingers of his right round mine. When the door unlocked with a click, Raiden took a deep breath and looked at me.

"This, my dearest William, is my hoard."

His hoard.

I hadn't really thought about that before, even though he'd mentioned multiple times that he considered Cam and I a part of his hoard. And all the dragon legends portrayed them as creatures who hoarded gold and jewels and protected the treasures with their lives. Somehow, it still hadn't completely clicked that my Raiden was one of those creatures. Even though I'd seen him in his full dragon glory.

But when Raiden led me through the secret entry into his hoard stash and the lights flicked on, it finally sunk in.

The room wasn't huge. It was about the size of the master bath in my house with a high ceiling and a warm yellow light shining from overhead.

The room displayed wall to wall and floor to ceiling shelving, but other than that, the only furniture was a single-person dark-brown reclining sofa, a wooden side table with a pile of books on it, and a small ottoman. Did Raiden come here to read? In the middle of all this?

I looked at Raiden to find his eyes glittering. Unlike their usual stormy color, they were almost metallic at the moment. Like liquid mercury. Or silver.

I turned back, examining the room. I walked over to the shelf nearest to me. It held gold, silver, and jeweled pieces that I couldn't even imagine the price of. This was a hoard, alright.

Arms wrapped around me, and I leaned back into Raiden as my eyes roamed over all the glittering pieces of jewelry.

"Wow . . . you have so many of these. And some of them look . . . ancient."

Raiden chuckled, his warm breath on my ear making me shiver. "You do make me feel so old, William." I'd noticed he had the tenancy to date himself with old English when he was feeling emotional, and I found the quirk so damn endearing.

I looked back at him, smirking. "Well, you're definitely older than me. And yet, I'm the one who looks like he's preying on someone much younger." I was exaggerating, of course. There was no mistaking the wealth of wisdom that he exuded. Raiden rolled his eyes at that, looking more like the twenty-something he appeared to be.

My smiled quickly morphed into a shocked gulp as I watched in wonder while his blond hair became peppered with gray strands and laugh lines formed around his eyes. In just moments, he looked ten, maybe fifteen, years older than he had. "Is this better, my love?"

That was the second time he'd called me that, and I realized that as unlikely as I'd thought it'd be, I was in love with him too.

Raiden may be a storm dragon, but he'd brought nothing but sunshine and warmth into my and Camille's life. After a long time of only thinking about my daughter, Raiden had made me think about myself, about what I needed. And I needed him.

"William?" Raiden's voice was softer now, more hesitant.

I smiled at him as I turned completely around in his arms so we were face-to-face and placed my palms on his cheeks, pulling his face closer to mine.

"I don't need you to change in any way or form, Raiden. You're perfect just the way you are. I . . . I love you just the way you are."

I swallowed Raiden's surprised gasp in a kiss, and my fingers sank into his hair as I pulled him closer still. I kissed him deeply, wanting to taste all of him.

Our bodies pressed as close to each other as physically possible, and yet, it wasn't enough. It was as if my soul was reaching out to Raiden's, trying to join with its other half and be whole again. Raiden had explained fated mates to me before, but until now, I hadn't actually realized the depths of the bond. But now I did.

Because underneath my own desire and love for this beautiful creature, I could feel a deep sense of peace and yearning, want and love. Emotions that I felt too but weren't mine. They were Raiden's. I could sense him in my heart because he was my other half.

I walked Raiden backwards, still kissing him as my palm roamed over his back, tracing the firm expanse of it. His skin was warm and smooth under my hand, and I wanted to touch more of him. I wanted to touch all of him.

I pulled away from the kiss when I remembered I needed to breathe, and seeing we were close enough to the recliner, I pushed Raiden back into it.

He squawked as he fell back and stared up at me with wide eyes. "William!"

I chuckled at the undignified squeak before straddling him. I pecked his nose before pulling back to look into his quick-silver eyes. "Is this okay?" I asked, grinding down into him to emphasize my point.

His eyes widened even more, and he swallowed hard. "Shouldn't I be the one asking that, my love? Since this is your first time with a man?"

I smiled at him, my heart jumping around in my chest like an overexcited puppy. "The idea of having sex with you has never been anything but wonderful, Raiden. All my hesitance had been because . . . because I hadn't felt at peace about my relationship with Veronica. I know I haven't been with a man before, that I'm completely inexperienced, but I'm not scared of it. I want to share everything with you, Raiden. My love, my daughter, my heart, my soul, and my body. It's all yours, just like you're all mine."

Raiden's eyes welled up at my words, reminding me of the way the skies were reflected in the lake earlier today. "Oh, William." Then he pulled me in and kissed me. Hard. It was lips and tongues and even some teeth. It was heady and full of desire. It was everything.

I could feel every inch of Raiden, but it wasn't enough. There were too many clothes, not enough skin. I pulled back from the kiss and started unbuttoning Raiden's shirt. Even though I'd told him to dress comfortably for our date, he'd worn a button-down dress shirt and slacks that clung to his legs oh-so-perfectly. But that also meant it took me way too damn long to open his shirt.

I pulled my shirt off, before pushing his off his shoulders and it was only then that I really took in his bare chest. How had I never noticed this before? I'd never seen him shirtless before, that's why.

In awe, I ran my fingers down his torso, tracing the slightly raised skin. It wasn't as smooth as the rest of him. It was . . . leathery, and the pattern resembled his scales in dragon form. His skin even had a sheen to it, as if it were dusted in sliver.

"Ray, you're beautiful. I can't believe you're all mine."

Raiden let out a shuddering breath, and I looked up into his eyes, though my fingers continued tracing the beauty of his skin. He looked . . . wary. Did he think I wouldn't like what I saw?

"The skin . . . it's a symbol of the dragon magic that courses through my veins. In any form I take, it's the same. A reminder of where I come from."

"It's beautiful, Ray. All of you is."

Raiden gave me a small, shy smile, and I realized sometime during our make-out session, he'd lost the grays and the laugh lines. I also realized that I loved him just the way he was: a shy two thousand-year-old disguised as a twenty-something with the most beautiful gray eyes I'd ever seen.

I leaned closer to him and claimed his lips again as I trailed my fingers down his chest. I rubbed my palm over his crotch, and he jerked up into my hand, a low groan slipping past his lips.

I trailed kisses down his jaw, nibbling at his chin as my hand slipped beneath the waistband of his slacks. His erection was warm and heavy in my palm, and I pumped him slowly with just enough pressure to drive him crazy. I was inexperienced in the art of gay lovemaking, but I had an six-year PhD in pleasuring myself, and if I knew anything, it was how to play with a dick for maximum pleasure.

I sucked Raiden's earlobe into my mouth, running my tongue over it as he shuddered underneath me. "William, please." His fingers were tight on my hips as he begged.

I ran my tongue along the shell of his ear as I slipped my hand from his pants. Hooking my thumbs in his waistband, I pushed it down his hips, freeing his gorgeous cock. I needed more of that creamy skin on display, so I struggled with the fabric while trailing open-mouthed kisses down the vast expanse of his silver chest. Raiden, realizing the issue, nodded for me to stand. He lifted his hips, displaying the hard planes of his V cut as I helped him slide the slick fabric down his legs and off before discarding my jeans at his feet as well.

I swallowed, feeling self-conscious all of a sudden. The last person to see me naked had been Veronica, and that had been almost seven years ago. I wasn't the same man anymore. I was older and nowhere as fit as I used to be. I had padding on my stomach, and my muscles had lost their definition somewhere around the time I'd picked spending time with my daughter over going to the gym.

"Oh, William, I have no words to explain what you do to me." My eyes shot to his, sure he was teasing, but he wasn't. His eyes were heavy-lidded, his palm wrapped around his dick, and he was watching me like he wanted to devour me.

That one look, the desire in his eyes, made all my doubts disappear in an instant, and I wondered if it was his magic's doing or just him. It didn't matter.

I climbed back onto him, chuckling at the picture we made. Him, all lean and lithe muscles covered in smooth, silky skin, with me, big and very much a bear on his lap.

My hand latched back onto his dick as I claimed his lips in a searing kiss, then I grabbed my own dick so it was pressed against his warm, silky cock and pumped us together as I kissed him.

Raiden moaned, a sound that spread through me like warm honey, making my strokes faster and my tongue delve deeper into his mouth.

I heard a crack of thunder somewhere above us and distantly wondered if the poor residents of Mistvale will have to live in a constant thunderstorm for the next however many years we lived here. Because I knew right then that I never wanted to stop.

"William! Oh, my love, please!" Raiden babbled incoherently as I kissed his neck, his throat, any part of him I could get my lips on.

I could feel my orgasm approaching, and I quickened my pace, twisting my wrist at the end of each stroke. Raiden's hands tightened on my shoulders, and he arched up into me as a loud shout escaped his lips, spurting over his stomach just as I reached my climax.

I pressed my lips to his and cried out as I came, my skin tingling all over as warmth raced through me. I couldn't remember the last time I'd come so hard, and I kissed Raiden with zero coordination as I tried to catch my breath.

My eyes were closed, my forehead resting against his, and I never wanted to move. But then Raiden's fingers traced a pattern on my chest, and they felt . . . different.

My eyes fluttered open, and I blinked a few times before I could focus on his fingers. Then I spotted my chest and gasped as I sat up, almost falling off his lap in my haste. I grabbed his arms to steady myself and stared at my chest with wide eyes.

"What?" I mumbled as I pressed a finger to the raised skin. It was exactly like Raiden's, except mine had a brown sheen to it rather than silver. They were patterned all over my chest, scales like the ones on his. "Raiden?"

I looked up to find him watching me with tears in his eyes, and then he blinked, and a solitary tear trailed down his cheek. I wiped it away with my clean hand. My chest hurt at his tears, even though I could sense he was anything but sad.

"I didn't know," he whispered softly, and I gave him a questioning look. "I . . . I think you're a dragon now, William."

I . . . what? That couldn't be true, right? "I thought dragons were born, not made. Didn't you say you came out of an egg?"

Raiden nodded, his eyes roaming over my chest again before he met my eyes. "I did. But it seems that I didn't know everything. Please know I didn't mean to hide this from you. I had no idea this could happen. I've never met a fated dragon before. I'd assumed my mate would receive my immortality like a mage's mate does, but it seems like you've received my dragon magic as well."

"So, I'll be able to turn into a dragon?"

Raiden tilted his head from side to side. "Maybe. We'll have to try. And you'll need to train for a while before you can even think of flying. It took me twenty years to learn how to fly, but I think it'll take you less since I'll be able to teach you."

My mind whirled with all this new information, and I shook my head, trying to clear it. One thought was all it took, though, to make everything else disappear.

"What about Cam?"

Raiden's smile slipped a little before he shook his head. "She will get my immortality, that is for sure. As for the other things, let's go home and check, shall we?"

Home. That sounded about right.

"Home, then. And how about you find someone to help move all this? A dragon's hoard should be in his actual home, shouldn't it?"

Raiden's brows furrowed in confusion for a minute before realization struck, and his eyes widened. He blinked at me a few times before crushing me into a tight hug. "I love you."

"I love you too, my sweet dragon."

Raiden

"Wait!" I squeezed William's hand before dropping it and rushing over to the shelves. I could sense William behind me as he followed, and I took a deep breath as I reached the small chest I'd filled with my favorite pieces a few weeks ago.

I opened the chest and pulled out the chain that sat on the top, covered in a fine silk cloth. It was made of platinum, its color a mirror to some of my scales in my true form. A rectangular pendant hung from the chain, framing a bright green stone the color of William's eyes. I'd owned this chain for years, but it was only after I met him that I knew it was meant to be his.

I turned to William, the chain hanging from my fist. With a deep breath, I extended my arm, offering it to him—offering all of my hoard—to the man who owned my heart. "William,

I'd like you to have this as a symbol of my love for you and as a promise that anything that is mine is yours. This hoard, this house, my life, my body, my heart, it's all yours. And I know you will treasure all I am like I treasure all of you."

William smiled at me with a soft look in his eyes as he curled his fingers around my hand. "I'd be honored to wear it, Raiden. But I'll only accept it if you put it on me."

I smiled widely as he turned to face away from me, and I carefully put the chain around his neck, making sure it was secure before letting the clasp rest on the center of his neck. Usually, I tried not to be too possessive of him, but when he turned to me, gazing down at the emerald, the very sight of him wearing my jewelry made warmth spread through me, and only one word echoed through my head: mine.

"Shall we?" William asked and I nodded before turning around and grabbing the chest.

William quirked a brow at me when he spotted it, and I explained, "For Cam."

With a smile, he wrapped his hand around my free one, and we walked out of the vault. I couldn't believe William had so casually asked—or told, to be precise—me to move in with him, but it was all I'd wanted from the moment we met, and it took all my self-control to not start packing right this moment so I could be with my family without any delay.

William took the keys this time, but I smiled when he still opened the car door for me. The drive between our houses was short, and the moment we stepped into the living room, we were bombarded by questions.

"Dad! DD! You're back! How was your day? Did you have fun? DD, did you like the boat ride? What's in the box?"

"Calm down, sweetie. Can we maybe grab a glass of water before the inquisition starts?" William joked, even as Rose, his housekeeper, brought us glasses of water. I wondered if I could convince him to fire the woman, not because I didn't like her, but because having a clueless human in the house could be dangerous. Not to mention, it'd mean we would be unable to talk about anything supe related.

William must have seen something on my face or made the realization himself because he smiled up at the woman and said, "Hey, Rose. Take the rest of the week off, okay? We'll manage."

Rose smiled at Will, and I had to work to keep myself from scowling. I didn't want to look like a jealous lover, but I was having a hard time holding myself back.

"Actually, sir, I wish to resign. I'll be happy to work here until you find someone else, but my husband got a raise and is being transferred, so we need to move next month. I hope it's not too much trouble."

William glanced at me, and I nodded. Somehow, he'd concluded that we wouldn't be needing a nanny or a housekeeper anymore. Honestly, now that I'd found William and Camille, I had no desire to go back to work. Work had been a way to keep myself from becoming a hermit, a way to stay in society. It wasn't like I needed the money, and even if I did, my investments would keep earning me a pretty nice sum. And my manager took care of most things, anyway. I'd be more than happy to stay home all day, spending time with my family, taking care of the house.

After living alone for over two thousand years, I had no desire to spend even a moment away from these two.

"That's completely fine, Rose. We actually don't need someone else, so I'd be happy to pay you for next month without you having to come in. It's my way of saying thank you for all the ways you've helped me out over the years, so please don't say no."

Rose looked surprised, but then a smile spread across her lips, and she nodded. "Thank you, sir."

"Great. I'll have Avery take care of it."

Cam raced over to the woman and hugged her tightly, looking up at her. "I'll miss you, Rosie."

"I'll miss you too, sweetie. Be good for your dad, okay?"

Cam glanced over at us and grinned. "I'll be good for both of my dads, Rosie. I promise."

Dads. Could this day get any better?

After Rose had left, we told Cam all about our date—minus the intimate parts, of course—and it was only after we'd cooked and eaten dinner that my eyes fell on the chest I'd placed on the coffee table.

We were all cuddled up on the couch, watching one of Cam's favorite shows, and I turned to her.

"Camille, would you like to complete our bond?"

Camille looked up at me instantly while hitting the mute button on the remote. "Yes! What do I need to do?" She looked much better now than she had this morning, and I was glad.

I smiled at her and offered her my hand, palm up. "Can you hold my hand, please?"

She placed her palm on mine instantly, and I wrapped my fingers around hers. William watched from her other side, a soft smile on his lips.

"We don't have to do anything complicated. I've already accepted you as a part of my family, my hoard. All you need to do now is accept me as part of yours."

Cam's blue eyes shined brightly as she beamed at me. "You're my father just as much as Dad is, DD. You're my family, and

I love you. I'll always respect you as I respect Dad. And even when I make a mistake, I know you'll always take care of me."

"I will, my sweet Cam. I vow to protect you and keep you safe for as long as I'm alive." I watched Cam's face carefully as I felt the magic flicker down my arms and into our joined hands. It raised the hairs and sent gooseflesh racing across her bare forearms. Her eyes widened and so did her smile, though I'd thought it would be impossible for a person to smile any wider.

"Oh," she mumbled, then pulled her T-shirt away from her chest and peeked inside.

"DD, what's happening? Why is my skin . . ."

"It's okay, sweetie. It happened to me too. Apparently, our dear dragon didn't know that bonding with us might turn us into dragons too."

"What?" Cam screeched, her eyes lighting up with excitement. "I can turn into a dragon?"

"Maybe. I'm not sure," I said and Cam jumped to her feet.

And before I could say anything else, magic swirled in the air, a warm tingle that felt as familiar as my own magic but was just a touch different, unique to our daughter. And where Cam had stood only a moment ago, now a beautiful purple dragon stood. Barely five feet in dragon form, her purple scales seemed to glimmer in the artificial light, her face splitting into a toothy dragon grin as her tail whipped around, almost hitting poor Snuffles in the side as he stared up at her with a lolling tongue. Cam was simply majestic. Familiar blue eyes twinkled at us as William walked closer to her, an awed look on his face.

"Children are able to shift more easily," I breathed, having forgotten my youth when I'd shift into different animals throughout the day just because changing forms had been so effortless at that age.

Cam made a soft chirping sound and slid closer to me. I wrapped my arm around her, careful of her shiny scales, and William did the same.

This. This was what I'd been looking for. A family. And after two thousand years of searching, I finally had them.

Epilogue

Around two years later | A few months after the events of Claws.

William

I walked into the house to the familiar sounds of my daughter and my husband chattering in the kitchen, and a smile spread across my lips as I removed my shoes.

We'd gotten married a year ago, in a courthouse with Jai and Raphael as witnesses. Being a dragon, the idea of marriage hadn't had much meaning to Raiden, and I hadn't wanted a ceremony either. Our main goal for getting married had been so Raiden could adopt Cam more easily. Well, he'd also told me he could fake papers if I didn't want to get married, but I liked wearing his ring on my finger.

"What have my dragons been up to?" I asked as I stepped into the kitchen. Cam looked up from where she was sitting on the kitchen counter and grinned at me, though there was something off about it. She looked . . . nervous?

"Hey Dad, welcome home! DD and I practiced flying today! Well, he only let me jump off the balcony, but I managed to fly a bit without crashing."

I shook my head at her. She'd been practicing with Raiden for the past two years, and he'd insisted that he would only teach her how to fly once she'd mastered her shifting. Well, now she had.

I walked over to Raiden, who stood at the stove, and wrapped my arms around him. He smiled as he sank into me, and I held him as I kissed his cheek. "Hey, beautiful. What are you making?"

After a month of living with us, Raiden had declared that he was done with work. He'd sold his investment firm because he said he had enough money for the next century and he wanted to be a househusband. I'd thought about arguing that he didn't need to give up his work for us, but then he'd spent a week at home, and I'd realized he loved it. And how could I ever stop him from doing something he loved?

And so here he was, a two-thousand-year-old dragon living the life of a househusband and taking care of our daughter while I was at work. He seemed to glow brighter every day.

"Cam's favorite," Raiden said, answering my question.

"Oooh, anything special happen today?" I asked, turning to Cam who looked even more nervous now. Her whole demeanor was starting to worry me. She ran her fingers through her hair—she'd preferred to keep it short once it had grown back after the cancer treatments—and took a deep breath before facing us.

"Dad, DD, can I talk to you both before dinner?"

Like me, Raiden sensed the seriousness of the situation and set the microwave timer before turning to Cam as I uncrossed my arms and gave our daughter my full attention.

"Of course, sweetie. How about we take this to the couch?"

Cam nodded, and we walked into the living room. I sat down on our couch and pulled Cam beside me. Raiden immediately slid in on her other side, like we usually sat for movie times, and I turned to her.

"What is it, sweetheart? You know you can tell us anything."

Cam nodded and blew out a breath. She grabbed my hand in one of hers, and then she grabbed Raiden's with her other.

"Micah said you guys won't react badly, and I know you won't, but I'm still scared because stupid society makes you think you're doing something wrong when you're just trying to be yourself." Micah was Gus and Cassian's son, and he and Cam had grown pretty close over the past few months.

"Are you two dating?" I asked and the face Cam made had me chuckling.

"I guess that's a no, then."

"Yeah, no. Dad!" She shook her head, as if trying to get rid of the thought.

"It's not that. It's just . . . I'm . . . God, this is harder than I thought it'd be . . ." She squeezed our hands tightly, and I looked at Raiden over her head, meeting his worried gaze. What was up with our daughter?

"I'm not a girl!" she shouted, startling us both. Then, in a much softer voice, she repeated, "I'm not a girl."

She looked at me and then at Raiden. I had no idea what face I was making, but I hoped she could sense that I supported her. Maybe she could sense it because she continued, "I'm a boy. And I know . . . I know I'm super young, but I'm not wrong about this, I promise. I've felt off for a long time, but I just didn't know what it was until some time ago."

I turned her—him so he was looking at me and said, "I'll only ask this once, not because I doubt you, but just because I'd like to hear it. Are you sure?"

Cam's eyes watered and he nodded. "I am. I . . . I look all wrong, but in here"—he patted his chest—"I'm a boy."

Raiden put his hand on Cam's shoulder. "Then that's all that matters, sweetheart. We love you. We loved you when we believed you to be our daughter, and we'll love you now that we know you're our son. It changes nothing." My love for Raiden grew even more as he spoke, and I was sure I had a dopey grin on my face.

"Well, it changes some things," I said, winking at Cam when s—he gave me a worried look. "Like, we can actually have opinions now when we take him shopping. And we can teach him how to shave."

Cam gasped softly before throwing himself at me, his arms wrapping tight around my neck as he buried his face in my chest. "I love you, Dad."

Then he did the same to Raiden. "I love you, DD."

He pulled back, got up, and took a seat on the coffee table so he was facing us. He'd dropped his hands and was now wringing them together.

"Cam, we'll support you with whatever you need," I said. "You know that, right? And can I still call you Cam? Would you prefer a different name?" Cam smiled at my barrage of questions, but he also relaxed a little, so I considered it a win.

"You can call me Cam, Dad. I don't mind the name. Actually, I like my name a lot. But can we maybe switch to Camillo instead of Camille?"

"Whatever you want, Camillo," Raiden said softly, and I nodded in agreement.

Cam laughed softly, shaking his head. "You're taking this so well."

"Did you think we wouldn't?" Had I really made my kid feel like he couldn't come to me?

"Of course not, Dad! I knew you guys would be okay with it, but it's just . . . kind of an ingrained thing, I guess. I made some trans friends online while I was trying to figure things out, and most of them had at least one or more members in their family who didn't understand them."

I nodded as I understood what s—he was saying. I could understand the fear of the unknown.

"You'll have to tell us some things, sweetheart," Raiden said. "We'll probably make mistakes along the way, but I promise we'll be there for you and do anything you need, okay?"

I couldn't have said it any better than him, so I just nodded my agreement.

"I want to start treatments. I couldn't research much, but I know what I want. I need your help with it so I can have the body I want."

"Anything," I promised, glancing up at Raiden for his agreement, only to find him watching Cam with a thoughtful look on his face.

"Raiden?"

"Tell me, Cam, this treatment. It's so you can have a male body, yes?"

Cam raised a brow as he watched Raiden but nodded.

Raiden smiled, a wide, brilliant smile. "Then perhaps we'll need to push back our flying lessons."

"What? Why?" Cam demanded, shooting to his feet.

"Because, my sweet Cam, you're a dragon. You don't need treatments to be the way you wish to be."

Cam stared at Raiden for a long moment before his eyes widened. "You mean . . ."

It took me a moment longer to understand what he was saying, but then I remembered the day we'd met and how Raiden had told me he could turn into a woman if that's what I wanted in my partner. "Oh!"

Raiden smiled. "It'll take less time than the treatments, and you'll have more control over your changes."

"And it'll be permanent?" Cam asked, his eyes full of hope and excitement.

Raiden nodded. "And I also have the power to change what someone else looks like. It's not permanent, but I'd be happy do it until you've learned to do it yourself."

Cam squealed, telling me nothing had changed except his name and pronouns, before throwing himself at Raiden, repeating the same two words again and again: "Thank you."

I slid over and wrapped my arms around them, effectively making it a group hug. When I'd lost Veronica, I'd never expected to find love again, and yet here I was. My family was complete, and I couldn't imagine being happier than this.

I may not have embraced my newfound dragon as easily as my son had, but I was looking forward to spending forever with the two boys I loved. My hoard. My family.

Camillo

I leaned against the doorway as I watched my dads and smiled. They sat on the couch, talking softly as Dad played with DD's fingers. I was so lucky to have them.

The way they'd reacted to my confession had left me in awe. All my trans friends online had at least one family-related horror story about their coming out, and though I knew my dad and DD loved me, I'd still been nervous about telling them. But they'd taken it all in stride, and DD was even going to teach me how to change my body so I could be myself without having to go through treatments and surgeries. I mean, how cool was that?

I'd seriously lucked out in the parents' department. I didn't remember much about my mom, but Dad had told me she'd been a fierce, kind woman who didn't take crap from anyone and loved Dad with her whole heart. And Dad himself had been my rock since I was a baby. And now I had DD, someone who loved me and my dad with his whole heart. What more could I ask for?

I blew out a breath, feeling relieved and freer than I ever had. I walked over to my dads, and they made space for me between them, like I'd known they would. And I grinned as I cuddled up to them, now surer than ever that my family would always be there for me.

I was Camillo Hawthorne-Raine, a trans dragon-boy, and my story was just beginning.

Also By Stella

PARANORMAL ROMANCE

Set in Mistvale

Mages of Ravenshire:
Set in the fictional town of Mistvale, Mages of Ravenshire is a series filled with magic, laughs and love. Low on angst and high on sweetness, Mages of Ravenshire will leave you with a smile on your face. Come meet Neya, Pads, April, and all the other fur-babies and their humans, vampires and mages.

Touch of Magic. (Goofy mage x nerdy human)

Sleep of Eternity. (Grumpy mage x sunshine vampire)

Angel of Death. (Sweet necromancer x snarky vampire)

Boxset. (With a special bonus scene.)

Misfits of Mistvale:
With side-characters from Mages of Ravenshire, this series features shifters, half-mermen, werewolves, and many more supernaturals. With the usual dose of fur-babies, found family, and all the Mistvale feels, this series features standalones with a different couple in each book.

Claws. (Graysexual bobcat x cat shifter)

Tails. (Merman-siren x dolphin shifter)

Bonds. (Human x femme wolf shifter x asexual werewolf)

Mistvale Spin-Off Novellas:
Featuring various side-characters from the town of Mistvale, these novellas are full of sweet, fuzzy romance, and the meddlesome cast of Mistvale.

My Elf Mate. (GFY, holiday, elf x wolf shifter.)

<u>My Dragon Mate</u>. (Bi-awakening, human x dragon.)

<u>My Elf Daddy</u>. (Daddy/little, elf x human.)

<u>My Fae Mate</u>. (Genderfluid MC, holiday, Fate x Alchemist.)

<u>Make A Wish</u>. (Djinn x Human, free read.)

Set in Otherworld

Fate's Gambit Trilogy:
Fate's Gambit is an MMM PNR trilogy featuring a sweet, subby cinnamon-bun devil, a gentle-giant who's a service sub/Daddy switch, and a slightly frustrated Master as they slowly figure our their dynamic and fall madly in love. They're joined by annoyingly awesome side-characters including a sweet hedgehog, a sassy talking snake, and a guardian in the form of a cat-man. This trilogy features the same triad and needs to be read in order.

<u>First Play</u>. (Free Prequel.)

<u>Devil's Gamble</u>.

<u>Pet's Ploy</u>.

<u>Master's Design</u>.

<u>Boxset</u>.

Lords of Otherworld:
Following the events of Fate's Gambit, Lords of Otherworld delves deeper into the workings of Otherworld, with new characters, new romance, and new adventures. With found family vibes, danger and romance, each book in this series follows a different couple, with an overarching storyline. It is recommended to read the books in order.

<u>Maximus</u>.

<u>Zane</u>.

<u>Nox</u>.

Standalones

<u>Elijah Summons A Demon</u> (A newsletter serial.)

CONTEMPORARY ROMANCE

Voice Out

<u>Weathering The Storm</u> (Roommates to lovers, hurt/comfort.)

<u>Watching The Sunrise</u> (Friends to lovers, genderfluid MC.)

About Stella

Stella Rainbow lives in a small town in India with her family and her five-year-old cat, Harry, who is her number one supporter, cuddle buddy, and writing buddy all rolled into one.

Living with a chronic illness, Stella grew up with books as her best friends, and now she writes in the hopes of giving others like her a reprieve from the real world.

Stella's books are low on the angst, high on the sweetness, with a doze of found family, and some absolutely adorable fur—and sometimes scale—babies.

You can join her <u>mailing list</u> to receive updates about her books and free content. You can also read more about Stella, her books, and the universe she writes in on her website, <u>www.authorstellarainbow.com</u>.

You can also follow her on:

Facebook: <u>Stella Rainbow</u>
Instagram: <u>@authorstellarainbow</u>

Goodreads: <u>Stella Rainbow</u>
BookBub: <u>Stella Rainbow</u>
Amazon: <u>Stella Rainbow</u>

www.ingramcontent.com/pod-product-compliance
Lightning Source LLC
Chambersburg PA
CBHW031425130726
47989CB00003B/1030